Whom were they planning to kill?

Isabel's heart beat furiously as she stood by the door, listening to the clan chieftains inside. She could scarcely believe her ears.

The topic of discussion was a ruthless plot that, if successful, would throw the whole of Scotland into a furor.

Isabel tiptoed away, realizing it was her duty to bring news of this treachery to the king, yet miserable at the thought of the consequences.

For one of the traitors she would send to his death was the man she loved!

Black Fox

KATE BUCHAN

A MASQUERADE HISTORICAL FROM

WORLDWIDE

TORONTO • LONDON • NEW YORK

For Pam and Nigel

Masquerade Historical edition published April 1980
ISBN 0-373-30038-7

Originally published in 1979
by Mills & Boon Limited

Printed in Canada

CHAPTER
ONE

LONG purple shadows from the high ridge of Ben Bhreac were already lying across the grass as Isabel Douglass slipped out of Strathblair Castle and made her way into the cool haven of her little herb garden. She took a deep breath of the sweet-scented air and glanced thankfully up at the high mountains behind the castle, where the evening sun still gilded and lit the last of the glowing heather.

It was hot and overcrowded in the great hall of the castle and she had left her place at the high table at the first moment she decently could, grateful for the peace outside after the noisy crude laughter of the men.

For days they had been assembling; ever since word had come that Isabel's, father, the Earl of Strathblair, had finished his business with the king at last and was returning home to the north. They were boisterous, confident that his return would mean another raid south for some long-delayed fighting and the chance to win themselves some rich booty.

The Earl had been expected daily for the last week, but the long road through the pass to the south remained empty of horsemen. Isabel glanced over her shoulder to where the main gate of the castle faced out towards the mountains. It was screened from where she stood by the tall rowan, heavy with scarlet fruit, which grew in the angle of the high wall sheltering her herbs from the cruel east wind. There was a good crop on the tree this year; she would have to see that the berries were gathered before the birds stole every one from the tree. She was standing on the damp grass watching the antics of a greedy mistle-thrush, gorging itself on the fruit, when out of the corner of her eye she saw something move in the shadows beneath the tree. She tensed nervously.

A man swathed in a dark cloak was standing half hidden, watching her. She felt her heart give a quick lurch of fear and she glanced round quickly, looking for one of her father's men, but the castle courtyard was deserted. The guards on duty were all on the walls, looking out towards the hills and too far away from her anyway to be of use if she called them.

She took a hesitant step backwards, towards the safety of the doorway, her eye warily fixed on the dark figure beyond the tree. As soon as she moved, the man stepped forward. The glow from the setting sun fell full on his face at last, and she gave a gasp of recognition. For a moment she was too surprised to move, then overcome with sudden happiness she ran towards him, her hands outstretched to meet his.

"Andrew? Oh, Andrew, is it really you? When did you come back?" Careless of any eyes that might have been watching from the high granite walls behind her, she flung herself into his arms.

"So you do remember me, little cousin?" His voice was gentle as for a moment he folded her into his embrace. Then almost guiltily he pushed her away and held her at arms' length, looking at her.

"Remember you?" She stared up at him, a little hurt. "Andrew, what do you mean?"

He had changed hardly at all in the two years since he had gone away and left her. His fair hair was perhaps a little fairer, his face tanned to a darker brown by the hot southern sun, but his eyes were the same, a deep smoky grey – the eyes of a poet and a dreamer; the eyes of the man about whom she had thought constantly and with an aching longing ever since he had announced that he was off to seek his fortune in France.

So short a time it had taken, between the telling and the parting. He had left her quickly one golden spring morning, with a smile and a kiss on her hand and a promise for the future when he would no longer be a poor suppliant at her father's table. He had been so proud, her Andrew. Poor and proud, and very much in love.

"I thought you would have found yourself another

suitor by now, my Isabel." He smiled gently at her. "Two years is a long time for the beautiful daughter of the Earl of Strathblair to remain unwed." Then his eyes grew sad again. "I'm afraid I never made that fortune, my dear. I am still too poor to ask for the hand of Isabel Douglass. The French king's court liked the poems of a simple Scots poet and he even gave me a purse of silver, but that was all, so I had to travel his kingdom like a troubadour of old. I've ridden the length of England as well. I've sung and written and recited nearly half-way across the world, but I'm afraid I have come home to the glen without growing rich."

She was shaken for a moment by the wave of treacherous disappointment which overwhelmed her at his words. But, almost at once she was herself again. She looked up into his face and gave a little smile.

"Andrew, I don't care. I've never cared about your being poor. I told you that before you went. You are my father's kinsman, surely that is enough?" She took his hands longingly in hers, her eyes pleading. "Our King James is a poet too, Andrew. Maybe he would find a position for you at court?"

Andrew laughed a little bitterly. "Maybe. But scarcely a great enough one to support an earl's daughter."

She pulled away from him, suddenly angry. "Andrew, if you love me still, why do you keep making excuses?" In her agitation she took two or three paces away from him towards the beds of soft earth. She broke a sprig of lavender from a bush near the wall and crumbled the soft pale leaves between her fingers, then she swung round to face him again. "I shall think in a minute that you no longer want to marry me."

She tried to keep her voice light, but she was frightened by the new gravity in his face. When he had ridden off to seek his fortune he had been carefree and young and full of laughter, confident that love would conquer the world; now she saw that indeed he had changed. He was quieter, more thoughtful and more bitter.

"I love you, Isabel." He said it very quietly. "I have declared my love for you through three kingdoms and I have returned to pledge it again. But . . ." he shrugged, "your father would never permit the match. I doubt if I should even dare to ask him."

"Then don't." She ran back to him impulsively, her hazel eyes glowing with hope and excitement. "We'll run away, Andrew! Once we're married Father can do nothing. I'll follow you anywhere, you know that. I don't need money or riches or jewels; I don't care where I live as long as it's with you."

He took her hands again, a little wistfully, looking down at the slim girl with her delicate high cheekbones framed in the fillet and veil of her head-dress. Her eyes were alive with hope and trust.

"He wouldn't care if I went, Andrew, not really," she rushed on. "My brother Ian is the one he cares about, not me. He's been to see the king again at Linlithgow about him – that's where he is now. You remember, before you left, the king captured Ian and said he would hold him hostage for Father's good behaviour? Well, he still holds him, as he holds hostages, so I'm told, to guarantee the good behaviour of many of the nobles of Scotland. And Father never married again. Ian is still his only heir. Don't you see? Whether he's succeeded this time in winning the king's confidence or not, it's only Ian he really cares about. Please take me with you."

He swallowed. "I wish I could take you, Isabel. Perhaps I would if I didn't love you so much. But how can I tear you away from your home with nowhere to go? I have no mother to care for you. No servants. No roof to call my own." He slammed his fist into the palm of his hand in sudden despair. "No, it's not possible. We must part until I have found something to offer you. Truly, love, it's the only way. If only you can wait for me?"

"Oh Andrew, of course I'll wait. I would wait for ever, my dear." She looked at him pleadingly. His face was set with a determination she had not seen there before. It frightened her; all at once she was overwhelmed with unhappiness. She could not bear to lose him again so soon. She flung herself at him with a sob, burying her face against his chest. His arm went round her, comforting and strong, and miserably she raised her face to his.

He was about to kiss her when the sound of a distant trumpet came echoing across the courtyard and into the garden from the castle walls, and he drew back.

She pulled away from him. "That must be my father," she whispered guiltily. "We've been waiting for his return from Linlithgow for days now." Her eyes filled with tears again. "Andrew, don't go yet. Please wait. At least see him first. See if he's still fond of you; he used to like you so much."

"I'll wait, Isabel, of course. I must seek his permission to go off again and," he grimaced, "his bounty too; but sweetheart, you must realise that being fond of me when I'm a vagabond poet is one thing; being fond of me when I'm a prospective suitor for your hand is quite another. He'd probably have me thrown off the top of the keep if he guessed that I have even glanced in your direction." He smiled wryly. "Now go, go in, love. You don't want to be found here alone with me. Go and greet you father."

"You promise you won't leave suddenly?" Her heart ached at the anguish in his eyes.

He shook his head. "I've told you, sweetheart. I couldn't. Not without saying goodbye. Have no fear of that, my Isabel."

He stood beneath the rowan tree and watched as, a slight graceful figure in her pale blue gown and flowing kirtle, she went, stooping a little with the weight of her unhappiness, across the grass towards the shadowy archway.

It was not until after Lord Strathblair had eaten and quenched his thirst that he called his daughter to the small solar behind the hall and dismissed his attendants so that he could speak to her alone. He was a tall man, broad-shouldered and sturdy in his mud-splashed court gown and the travelling cloak which he had not yet taken off. His deeply tanned face was lined with fatigue as he looked at her. Then he smiled sadly, reaching out to embrace her.

"Well, Isabel, at last we can speak alone. How are you, child? As you can see I have left your brother once again at the king's side. Ian sends you his greetings, and of course his love."

Isabel shivered a little at her father's tone. "Won't the king release him, Father? In spite of your promises?" She was still trying desperately to shut the thought of Andrew out of her mind and concentrate on her brother's plight.

Twelve years before, King James I of Scots had returned from a long captivity in England, bringing with him an English bride, English ideas of government and statecraft, and the unyielding determination to master his warring, unmanageable nobility. This he achieved with a combination of force and cunning. The Earl of Strathblair had been one of the most reluctant to bow his head beneath his king's firm rule, but the private feuds which he had pursued with a zeal bordering on exuberance had at last been quelled when the king had contrived to capture young Ian, the Earl's only son and heir, the child whose birth had killed Isabel's mother.

The Earl pulled himself wearily from his chair and went to stand near the fireplace, gazing thoughtfully into the smoke. Watching him, her eyes wide with silent sympathy, Isabel sank quietly on to a stool near him.

"Perhaps the king will relent, Father? You could see him again in the spring. He won't keep Ian from you for ever. He is a just man, with a little boy of his own. He knows you would keep your word once you gave it."

She meant it as a comfort, but her words seemed to flow past her father unheeded, for he gave no sign that he had even heard her. He kicked viciously at the burning peats, watching the glow intensify and redden for a moment. Then slowly he turned to her.

"Isabel, the king has agreed to release your brother. He is, as you say, a just man, but also a prudent one. He fears that our quarrel with the Crawfurds of Glencarnie may again flare up and disrupt the peace of the kingdom, as our friends out there are hoping at this very moment." He gestured behind him towards the hall where his men were slowly falling asleep over their wine. "He therefore demands certain further guarantees so that it should never happen again."

Isabel was sitting quietly, her long skirts spread round her in the thick heather stems which were strewn on the stone floor.

She looked up at her father, her face suddenly lightening with hope. "Then Ian can come home? Oh Father, I am pleased." Impulsively she jumped up and ran to kiss her father's cheek. "Whatever the guarantee I know you would give it – for Ian."

"Aye." He nodded his head as he gently disengaged himself from her. "Aye, indeed I would. Your brother's safety means everything to me." He frowned. "You love him as much as I, I think?"

She hesitated, frightened suddenly by the expression in his eyes. "You know I do, Father."

"And you would do anything in your power to help him yourself?"

She nodded, numbly, filled with foreboding.

He drew himself up stiffly, and rubbed his hand across his beard.

"I have agreed, Isabel, that you should be married as soon as possible to Sir Duncan Crawfurd of Glencarnie, to seal the new friendship between our families. The king insists on the match, and Sir Duncan has agreed. I am to ride back to Linlithgow tomorrow, at first light, and you must go with me to show I keep my bargain . . ."

He stopped and swung round at the anguished cry which escaped her lips. "No! No, Father, no. I couldn't. You can't make me. Not even to save Ian."

The Earl's face darkened with anger. "To save Ian I would do anything, my lady, anything, do you hear?"

"But I love someone else, Father." She looked away from him desperately, frightened by the sudden implacable determination in her father's face.

His mouth had tightened into a straight line. Then, imperceptibly it relaxed. "Of course! Our handsome poet, I'd forgotten about him. But lassie, he left here over two years ago and he never came back, did he?"

She gasped. "You knew? You knew we loved each

other?" She had never for one moment suspected that her father had guessed.

"Of course I knew; the two of you behaved like moon-struck calflings – and very pretty it was, as far as it went. It was lucky he left when he did because if he hadn't I would have had to send him packing. There could have been no future for you with that young man. The Lady Isabel Douglass does not marry a wandering poet!"

"The king himself is a poet, if you remember," she flared indignantly.

Her father laughed harshly. "That's hardly the same, Isabel."

"And Andrew is your kinsman; he has noble blood!"

"Maybe, but he's penniless and without position." His mouth snapped shut on the words as he swept past her to a table where there was a jug of wine left ready. Pouring some into a goblet, he swung round on her. "Forget Andrew Douglass, Isabel. You will not be seeing him again."

She stood completely silent for a moment, fighting the fear which was mounting every moment inside her; then she lifted her chin defiantly.

"I have seen him again, Father. He is in the castle now. He returned from his travels this very day, and," she added, suddenly desperate, "he intends to ask you for my hand."

Lord Strathblair set down his goblet with a bang which spilled wine all over the table. He controlled his temper with an effort. "So, he found his fortune, did he?"

She shook her head, unable to hide her misery. "No. He found no fortune, but he is going to court to seek a position from King James."

Her father nodded soberly. "He could do worse. I shall write a letter for him myself, but Isabel –" his face was strangely compassionate as he saw her barely controlled despair. "Lassie, you realise it can make no difference. Even if he had returned a rich man, I could have done nothing. You are pledged to Sir Duncan now. If you refuse to marry him, we lose all. My castles, my lands, probably Ian's life and my own as well."

There was a long silence as Isabel turned away to the high window and gazed out across the swiftly darkening river valley towards the barrier of mountains to the west. A gentle breeze stirred the veil of her head-dress and unconsciously she raised her hand to straighten it, twisting the fine gauze around her fingers.

She felt her father's arm round her suddenly. "Remember you are a Douglass, my Isabel. You have the blood of warriors in your veins. You must have the courage to do what is required of you by your king. Remember, we are loyal to him above all else."

With a gentle pressure on her shoulders he released her. She heard the rustle of his gown on the heather as he strode across the room and he had gone, pulling the heavy door closed behind him.

She stayed a long time, gazing out of the window, watching the last carmine streaks disappear from the clouds above the blackening mountains; waiting for the silent mists which crept soft-footed up the shadowy corries, drawing in the darkness. She didn't cry. Her heart was too numb. She could not even think clearly. All she could do was gaze at the scene before her, dimly aware that she might never again see the night coming in from this window.

She heard the door opening behind her at last and saw the flickering light of a candle leaping on the walls as someone came into the room.

"Lady Isabel?" The hesitant voice of her own maid, Marjorie, broke into her misery. "Lord Strathblair has sent me orders to pack your coffers, my lady," the girl faltered. "He says I'm to go with you in the morning to the king's palace at Linlithgow."

Marjorie was a plump, usually cheerful girl, a little younger than Isabel, her pink cheeks and creamy skin betraying the bright red hair which her head-dress concealed. Her blue eyes were full of puzzled excitement as she looked at her mistress's taut narrow shoulders framed against the darkness of the embrasure.

Slowly Isabel turned to her at last. She forced herself to smile, and nodded. "My father is taking us, Marjie. It appears that I am to be married." Her voice came out as a broken whisper.

Marjorie stared at her in dismay. "But my lady! What about your Andrew?" she protested shrilly.

She had listened so often to Isabel's whispered dreams about the man she loved that she could not believe her own ears. "You can't marry someone else. Why, he's down there now!" She gestured behind her furiously towards the hall.

"I know." Isabel hid her face in her hands. "I still love Andrew, Marjie. I'll never, never, love anyone else. But what can I do? I have to obey the king and my father. I have to, for the Lord Ian's sake. Don't you see? I have no choice."

Marjorie pursed her lips. "And who's going to tell your Andrew that, may I ask?" she enquired tartly.

Biting her thumbnail anxiously, Isabel glanced over her shoulder at the blackness beyond the window. A brisk wind had sprung up, gently moving the heavy tapestries which hung on the walls.

"Where is my father, Marjie?" she asked suddenly, swinging round.

"He's with his steward, my lady."

"Quickly then. Fetch Andrew here. I must see him, now, before it's too late. I must be the one to tell him myself."

She watched wretchedly as, setting down the candlestick, Marjorie hurried from the room, leaving her alone in the guttering light. Then she walked slowly over to the window and leaned with her elbows on the deep sill, looking out at the evening star which had appeared in the limpid night sky.

In her mind she was hearing again the words which she had spoken such a short time before. "I'd wait for you for ever . . ." she had said to Andrew. For ever.

She put her head in her hands and began to weep.

When at last he came to her his face was very grave. "I shouldn't be here, Isabel. Your father would be very angry to find us alone together." He glanced over his shoulder, but Marjorie had already gone, closing the door softly behind her.

In a moment Isabel was in his arms. He held her tightly, kissing her on the lips and the chin and the forehead, then reluctantly he pushed her away.

"What is it, sweetheart? What's happened?"

As she raised her eyes to his in the dim flickering light of the single flame he saw there were tears still wet on her lashes.

She clung to him. "I have to go away, Andrew. I can never marry you. The king has ordered me to marry Sir Duncan Crawfurd of Glencarnie – at once."

For a moment he didn't move or speak, then he swore terribly under his breath, his arms tightening defensively around her.

"I'll never love him, Andrew; I'll never love anyone but you." She raised her face piteously to his again. "But I have to go. To save my brother." Her voice was trembling a little. "To save my father's lands and castles. You must not try to stop me. I have to go. There is nothing anyone can do about it."

He took a deep breath. "Perhaps after all it's best, Isabel." His voice was drained of emotion. "We both know I could never have made enough money or achieved the position needed to marry you. I am sure Sir Duncan will make you happy."

"He won't!" She turned on him passionately. "How can you say that? I shall hate him."

"You would have hated life with me more." He tried deliberately to keep his voice hard. "Love would have been enough for a while, then you would have started to miss your soft sheets, your pretty trinkets, your fine white bread."

She flinched at the callousness of his tone, taking a step back. "You know that's not true, Andrew," she flashed at him indignantly.

He knew, but he wasn't going to make it harder for her by pleading. He too was proud, and he knew she could do nothing to save herself from blackmail like this.

His handsome face was pale in the candlelight and his

mouth was set in a grim line as he looked at her for what might be the last time. Then he began to move away from her towards the door.

"I'll take my leave of you now, lady." He forced the words out, giving her a small, bitterly formal bow. "It's best this way. Quickly. I doubt if we will meet again."

"No! Andrew, please. Not yet. Wait!"

Neither of them noticed the door behind them opening as she threw herself into his arms again, sobbing.

The Earl of Strathblair stood on the threshold for a moment, his face thunderous, his hand on the hilt of his sword. Then with an oath he dragged the blade from its scabbard.

"What is this?" His voice, cold and harsh, cut like a whiplash through the sound of Isabel's weeping. With a strangled gasp she let go of Andrew, and without pausing to think she threw herself at her father's feet.

"Don't hurt him, please, please, Father. It's not his fault. I asked him to come and see me in here. He didn't even want to speak to me again. Please, Father, we were only saying goodbye." She was beside herself with terror for Andrew as the candlelight glinted on the naked blade between them.

The eyes of the two men met across the girl's head for an instant. The Earl's eyes blazed with suppressed anger whilst Andrew's were for a moment half blinded with misery and fear for Isabel. Then slowly Andrew drew himself upright. He was unarmed but he faced the Earl calmly.

"I am sorry that this should happen, my lord. But Isabel has made me see that she must do her duty and obey you for the sake of the family honour and for your son's sake. If it were not for that I would die rather than let you give her to Glencarnie." He clenched his teeth for a moment, then steadying himself with an effort he went on: "I just want her to know that if ever she needs me, or my sword," he glanced carelessly at the Earl's weapon, "I will be at her disposal until the day I die."

There was a moment's taut silence, then it was broken by the Earl's voice, trembling with anger. "Go, sir! Go.

Leave my castle. You are lucky that for her sake I did not kill you outright. You have compromised my daughter on the very eve of her betrothal." He thrust his sword angrily back into its scabbard, then he stepped aside, motioning Andrew out of the room past him with an angry gesture.

The younger man hesitated for only a moment. Then he went. He did not turn to look at Isabel. He could not bear to see again the anguish and fear in her eyes. His head held high, he ran down the steps out of her sight.

It was a long time before Isabel's sobbing subsided and she dared at last to raise her face to her father's.

"Get up, child," he said quietly. "Look, you've torn your gown." His voice still shook slightly as he held out his hand to help her rise. "Isabel, for your sake I shall let that young man stay here for the time being." He looked at the ground suddenly, a patch of colour rising in his face as if he were ashamed of the weakness he was showing. "He was greatly to blame for coming here alone to you, but . . ." He sighed, looking at her creamy skin, streaked with tears, and her great hazel eyes – so like her mother's. A strand of dark hair had slipped from beneath her head-dress and lay curling across her throat. If he had been a young man of Andrew's age, and in love . . . ! He scowled.

"No, there was no excuse for his coming here. You must never, never see him again. Do you hear?"

She nodded imperceptibly.

"I don't want you to think that I don't love you, child," he went on awkwardly. "It's just that a man needs a son; an heir . . ."

There was a moment's silence. Then he turned away from her towards the door. "Call your maid now, and go to bed," he finished brusquely. "It's long past the hour for retiring and we must ride early in the morning."

Wearily she climbed the spiralling staircase up towards the chamber she shared with Marjorie, her steps dragging as she fixed her eyes on the wildly leaping shadow of the candle as the girl preceded her upwards. Once she was there she sat down on the bed listlessly, unable to listen to Marjorie's determined chatter, or take any interest in the

packing of her coffers. All she could think about was
Andrew, with his gentle grey eyes and his last vow to her,
to be ready to serve her till the day he died.

Marjorie helped her undress, and then unfastened her
head-dress, beginning slowly to unbraid the long dark
hair, brushing out the silky tresses with an ivory-handled
brush, noticing with relief that the slow rhythmic strokes
seemed to soothe her mistress a little as she sat shivering
by the fire in her shift.

Isabel was just about to climb into the high bed at last
when there was a light tap at the door.

Marjorie threw down the brush and after an enquiring
glance at her mistress went to open it. There was a page
standing on the stone stair outside. He gave a little bow
and whispered to Marjorie, handing her something before
he turned and ran away.

Marjorie came back into the room and pushed the heavy
door shut. Her pink face was sad as she held out her hand
to her mistress.

"Something for you, lady." She was trying valiantly to
look cheerful.

It was a sprig of rosemary from Isabel's own herb garden.

"To remember," Isabel whispered, lifting the pungent
stem to her nose and smelling it with a sad little smile. "As
if I could ever forget him!"

CHAPTER
TWO

THEY left the castle early next morning, and try as she might Isabel could not catch even a glimpse of Andrew amongst the servants and retainers who were milling around the courtyard as she mounted her horse. She glanced up at the high windows of the keep, but there were no faces to be seen. Wherever Andrew was, he had not come to bid her farewell, and all too soon they were wheeling out through the opened gates and setting off at a brisk trot down the grassy strath towards the pass in the southern hills.

Lord Strathblair set a fast pace, and Isabel's horse was fresh from its stable. She leaned low over its neck and rode as hard as she dared. She had no more tears left; her eyes were streaming now from the cold wind which had sprung up overnight to usher in the autumn, and with her free hand she tried desperately to hold the hood of her cloak tightly round her head.

She had never before visited the king's palace at Linlithgow; never been to court at all, in fact. She had been only nine when her mother had died, and for the nine years that followed she had looked after one or other of her father's castles, turning it, wherever she was, into his home as if she were a grown chatelaine. Occasionally she had even had to look down, frightened but exhilarated, from the high keep, while her father's enemies, often the men of Glencarnie, came terrorising the glen and besieging their walls, and watched in an agony of excitement and fear when with wild whoops and howls of revenge the Earl and his men had at last burst from the walls of the castle and pursued their enemies from their lands with flashing swords.

It had been an enjoyable life, but it had never allowed

her the chance to visit outside her father's lands. Often she had dreamed of the glitter of the court and the thrill of travelling to meet the glamorous lords and their exotic ladies, but never had she guessed that when the day came at last she would find herself numb with terror and dread at what lay in store.

Their way led first through the lonely hills, where the escort of armed men spread out on the track before and behind them, the hoofbeats drumming a regular rhythm on the peaty ground, and then through thickly growing forests where the sunlight filtered through the entwined branches of oak and ash, and the men drew their swords, the sunbeams and shadows flickering on their armour, their eyes constantly scanning the undergrowth for hidden ambush.

The sun was setting in a blaze of stormy crimson in the western waters as they took ferries across the Forth and rode the last miles towards Linlithgow. By then, Isabel was drooping with fatigue, feeling herself leaning closer and closer to the neck of her dappled mare.

All day she had refused to let herself think about Andrew; the past was a bleak unhappiness she could not face, whilst a black shutter came down over her mind at the thought of the future. She just prayed over and over again that Sir Duncan had not waited for her and that their journey would have been in vain.

It was nearly dark when they at last rode round the dim mistiness of the loch towards the towering grey-yellow sandstone walls of the king's new palace of Linlithgow. Their escort reformed into a tight formation as they rode through the gates under the archway and into the Inner Close where they at last dismounted.

The palace was seething with people and noise, and Isabel gazed around her, dazed by the flickering blaze of lights, keeping close to her father, terrified lest he disappear and leave her amongst so many strangers. She was quite bemused by the crowds of richly-clothed men and women, huddled from the wind into their fur-trimmed cloaks, who all appeared at that hour to be hurrying in one direction – towards the king's hall.

Almost at once a bowing official appeared and guided them to guest rooms in the western range of the palace. Once there, her father kissed her goodnight at the door of her chamber, and disappeared to attend the king. Isabel, determined to hide her fears from Marjorie, ran to the high window and gazed out into the darkness towards the ruffled black waters of the loch and the invisible hills of her home.

· She slept hardly at all that night, tossing fitfully on the uncomfortable mattress, conscious of Majorie lying tensely on a pallet near her, her eyes staring up at the dark ceiling, watching and waiting for the dawn and the first notes of the thrush to echo eerily from the battlements somewhere high above.

She was up well before it was properly light, and Marjorie, groaning with stiffness after the long ride of the day before, helped her into her best gown of scarlet, worn over a kirtle of green. Then her hair was plaited and bound around her head beneath a fillet of gold with a silken veil falling delicately across her shoulders. She peered doubtfully at her image in the polished steel mirror which Marjorie held for her and smiled uncertainly.

"Am I fit to be seen by a king, do you think?" She rubbed her pale cheeks with her palms and bit her lips to make them redder. She had noticed that all the court ladies, the night before, had their faces powdered and their eyebrows and foreheads had been plucked bare beneath their elaborate head-dresses.

Marjorie laughed. "You'll outshine the court beauties easily, my lady." She tweaked Isabel's veil. "And your betrothed," she pursed her lips tightly, "will think himself lucky indeed when he sees you."

Isabel's cheeks paled again. "Please, Holy Mother, let him not be here still. Maybe he wants as little to do with me as I do with him. Maybe he will have gone home?"

"Maybe." Marjorie sounded sceptical. She stood back to admire her handiwork, pulling at the folds of the heavy scarlet train.

"Oh, Marjie," Isabel burst out suddenly, "I don't want

to see the king. I hate him for doing this to me. He must be an unfeeling, wicked man!"As Marjorie, with a nervous glance over her shoulder towards the door, hushed her desperately she went on, her voice rising passionately, "How could he force me into a marriage against my will, like this? It's against man's law and God's. It must be!"

She threw herself down on to the bed, in a swirl of scarlet and green, beating at the feather pillow with her fists.

"Hush, my lady." Marjorie was hovering over her anxiously when a loud knock on the door made her jump with fright. With a exclamation she scurried over to answer it.

A page stood outside, bowing, dressed in a livery of red and gold. "The Lady Isabel Douglass?" he asked. "I am here to show her to the king's presence."

Swallowing hard Isabel got up at once and straightened her skirts, then, holding herself proudly upright, she followed him, her hands playing nervously with the folds of her long gown as she walked, trying to ignore the cold terror which clutched at her stomach.

The boy hurried ahead of her down passages and up stairs, threading his way unhesitatingly through crowds of gaily-dressed courtiers, until at last they came to an antechamber near the chapel.

An usher came forward, bowing, "The Lady Isabel Douglass," murmured the boy and the man bowed again and beckoned her on.

Taking a deep breath she followed him into a small hall. A group of men were standing talking on one side of the room. Amongst them she at once recognised her father. She smiled with relief. She had been secretly terrified that he might already have left for home. He held out his hand when he saw her and then turned to one of the other men near him. Isabel caught her breath as her father bowed low.

"Sir, may I present my daughter Isabel?"

Trembling she went to take her father's hand. Then she curtseyed to the ground. The king was a man of middle height, dressed in a rich velvet gown sewn with pearls and trimmed with miniver, quite stocky in build and with a short greying beard, but his eyes were a piercing blue. They scrutinized her closely for a moment and then James held out his hand to her.

"Welcome, my dear. I see your father has not for once exaggerated in describing your charms. You are truly a beautiful flower amongst women."

She felt herself blush an unbecoming scarlet, curtseying again as the king continued to hold her hand. Then she saw his glance travel to the tall black-haired man standing alone by the window. "Come, Sir Duncan, are you not going to greet your bride?"

The colour drained from her face as she raised her eyes to look at him. He had a dark complexion and deep brown eyes, emphasised by his robe of nut-brown velvet, trimmed with gold thread. Almost casually he left the window embrasure and stepped up to the king's side. He bowed slightly.

"Your grace has done me a great service. I could have found no more beautiful bride had I looked myself for a thousand years." His voice was cold in spite of the gallant words.

Isabel gritted her teeth. She could feel herself beginning to tremble and she was determined not to betray her terror before the king, who was still holding her hand in a firm cool grasp.

In fact he had been about to hold her hand out to Sir Duncan, when he hesitated and turned to glance again at her face. His keen gaze saw through her proud façade at once and his expression softened imperceptibly.

To her astonishment he tucked her hand beneath his elbow and led her away from the others towards his chair and a table heavily loaded with books and documents at the far end of the room.

"You're afraid of him?" he asked bluntly, in a low voice.

She gulped nervously and then nodded, unable to pretend before that piercing look.

He pressed her hand. "You must try not to be. He's a handsome young man. A hot-head like your father there, but not unkind. Go to him doucely, lassie, and remember, I am your friend." He smiled at her kindly and beneath the warmth of his friendliness she felt all her resentment beginning to slip away in spite of herself. Instinctively she knew that here was a man she could trust. For a short moment he went on looking at her, and then he turned back to the others in the room. This time he did hold out her hand and he put it into Sir Duncan's with a courteous smile.

"Right. Now, Strathblair, when these two have left for Glencarnie, you shall have your son. Now leave me, all of you. I have work to do." With a dismissive gesture he turned to his table.

Isabel glanced up at the dour face beside her nervously and felt her throat constrict with fear at the expression she saw there. Sir Duncan's hand over her wrist where the king had joined them was set in an iron grasp and his features showed a barely concealed impatience. For a moment he stood looking thoughtfully after James without moving, and then he turned and began to walk determinedly towards the door.

She followed him meekly enough out of the king's presence, but then to her alarm he set off at once down the gallery in the opposite direction from that which her father was taking.

"I think we should get acquainted, lady," he commented curtly as she hesitated. His grip on her wrist did not slacken and she was forced almost to run with him as he made his way towards the far corner of the gallery where the queen's winding stair led down. He ran down it, pulling her after him, and then set off out of the great gateway and across the grass towards the lochside where an orchard of young fruit trees had been planted, their leaves already turning russet and gold in the chill wind. She shivered violently without her cloak, but Sir Duncan did not seem to notice. He did not slow his pace until they were some distance from the palace. Then abruptly he stopped and released her wrist.

For the first time he faced her, his dark handsome features not softening at all as he looked her up and down.

"So, this is the bride picked by the king for Crawfurd of Glencarnie. I hope, madam, you are worthy of the match." His tone was deliberately insolent and she felt her cheeks flame.

"A Douglass of Strathblair is worthy, sir, of the greatest in the land," she retorted. "I feel sure that *you*," she emphasised the word deliberately, "should be more than honoured."

Drawing her skirts round her fastidiously in the rustle of golden leaves she stepped away from him. To her surprise she heard him chuckle suddenly, "A spirited little cat, by God! Good. I should hate to be saddled with a snivelling mouse of a wife. The Black Fox of Glencarnie likes women he has to tame."

She shuddered at his words, but she continued to hold her head up high, trying to ignore him, gazing out across the slate-grey waters, her veil blowing round her face. Then he was beside her again and she was conscious suddenly of how tall he was, much taller than her father or Andrew.

At the sudden unbidden thought of Andrew tears pricked behind her eyes and she clenched her fists angrily, turning away from him to hide her face.

At once she heard the soft chuckle again. It sounded very sinister against the silent whispering of the wind in the apple boughs. "Do you refuse even to look at me, sweet Isabel? No matter. There will be time enough when we are married. I intend to leave court tomorrow, so you had better inform your father. No doubt he will be over-joyed, for then he will be able to retrieve his errant son, which I gather is all he waits for. I too have been kept dangling at royal Jamie's elbow. It has taken your timely arrival to earn his gracious permission to return to my own fireside." His voice was heavy with sarcasm. "And I intend to leave before he changes his mind. So," he reached out and caught her arm, swinging her to face him before she had time to step back, "repack your coffers, sweetheart. Tomorrow I take you to my mother at Glencarnie, and we will be married as soon as we can."

He looked at her for a moment, his dark eyes unsmiling

as they met hers, and then abruptly he turned and strode back up through the young orchards, leaving her shivering alone at the lochside.

In the great hall that night, seated at the feast between her father and Sir Duncan, the food before her cold and untasted on her plate, Isabel had at last seen her brother Ian again. He was dressed in the royal livery and waited as a page upon the king and his queen. He had grown plump and jolly during his time in the king's service and seemed anything but unhappy, putting up good-naturedly with his sister's hug for only a minute before he ran off. Of course, she told herself a little wistfully as he skipped away, he could not know what a sacrifice she was making for his freedom. She shrugged aside the thought, and the next time he came near her after the meal was over she grabbed his hand and pulled him into a corner.

"Can you keep a secret, Ian?" she whispered.

His eyes widened with excitement and he nodded quickly.

"Good. Listen, I want you to carry a letter back to Strathblair for me. To our cousin Andrew." She hesitated a moment and then rushed on. "You mustn't tell Father, Ian. There will be nothing wrong in the letter, but Father mustn't know about it. He would . . ." she shrugged helplessly. "Well, Father doesn't approve of my writing to Andrew even now that I am betrothed and it can't possibly matter any more. I didn't have the chance to bid Andrew goodbye. Not properly. Please, will you take it for me?"

It had upset her very much that she had not had the chance to speak to Andrew again after the scene with her father, and that he had not even put in an appearance to wish her Godspeed on the morning of her departure. His white face and pained determined eyes haunted her.

Ian grinned conspiratorially and nodded, then he ran off. She hadn't seen him again.

That night, when at last she had managed to escape from the hot candlelit hall, Isabel wrote the letter to Andrew. Marjorie procured writing materials from somewhere for her and a branch of candles and then withdrew, leaving her alone in the cold, silent little room.

She sat on the narrow window-seat with the candles glowing feebly in the sharp wind from Linlithgow Loch, trying desperately to think what to say. That she loved him; that she wanted him; that she would give up everything for him, even her honour and that of her father's house? She sighed bitterly. No, she could say none of that. It would only hurt him more.

"Good sir," she penned carefully. "Think no more about me. Tomorrow I go to Glencarnie where I am to marry Sir Duncan with the king's blessing. Be happy and know that I have done this for my brother whom I love and honour dearly. God guard you, my dear love, and farewell." She reread the letter slowly, her eyes full of tears, her hand shaking so much as it held the quill that a blot of ink fell on the page. She dabbed at it angrily and ran her hand across her eyes, dashing away the tears.

Unconsciously her fingers strayed to the neck of her gown. There, sewn inside her shift, was the sprig of rosemary. Carefully she freed it and held it for a moment in her cupped hands. Then, dropping a quick kiss on the spiky leaves, she folded it into the letter and pressed it flat. She must forget him, but perhaps if she returned his token with a kiss he would remember her a little in his heart, in spite of her brave instructions not to think of her again.

She wrote Andrew's name on the packet and found the sealing-wax Marjorie had brought with the pens. As they melted in the candle flame the drops of wax fell like blood on to the fold of the letter; then she pressed her ring into the wax, leaving the imprint of a flying dove, her own emblem. As she waited for the wax to harden she heard, somewhere in the distance, a faint rumble of thunder.

Marjorie had been waiting outside the door. She took the letter at once and pushed it into the bosom of her gown. "You rest, lady, I'll give it to your brother." She glanced at Isabel's red-rimmed eyes and tightened her lips grimly.

"Marjie, take care he remembers it's a secret," Isabel begged, catching the girl's arm. "He mustn't show it to Father. There's nothing wrong in it. I've only said –" she paused, a catch in her voice. "I've only said goodbye, but Father might be angry and punish Andrew – or Ian himself if he found out."

"Don't worry, I'll tell him." Marjorie's voice was surprisingly firm. "Now, you start preparing yourself for bed, my lady. I'll be back to help you as soon as I've found Lord Ian."

She turned and hurried off down the dark corridor, leaving Isabel to shut the heavy oak door and lean wearily against it, her eyes closed against the dim candlelight.

Marjorie found Ian at play with two other pages in the nearly empty hall; she caught his arm and pulled him protestingly out into the passageway.

"Now, listen to me, my lord, and listen well," she threatened the boy in a low voice. "Do you value your sister's life?"

Ian turned and stared at her, his eyes wide. "What do you mean? I love Is'bel."

"Aye, you love her. Do you know what she has done for you?" Marjorie's face was pink and very earnest, close to his in the dark passage.

He shifted uncomfortably. "I don't understand. She hasn't done anything for me, has she?"

Marjorie snorted. "Indeed she has. She's agreed to marry a man she hates and fears so that you can go back to Strathblair with your father. That's what she has done for you."

Ian gasped, his ears growing red. "I . . . I didn't know."

"No. Well, that's not your fault. You're too young to be your own master yet awhile, but you can help her and help her you must. Here." She groped in the neck of her gown for the letter and held it out to him. "Take this and give it to Andrew Douglass. Now listen. I don't know what my lady has written in that letter, but you must give him a message yourself. I wish I could write, but I can't, so you

must remember it. See? Once you're home, you're safe.
The Earl and my lady have kept their side of the bargain
with the king. If anyone else interferes with their plans it's
not their fault. That's the way I see it. Tell Andrew that.
Tell him that my lady has gone to Glencarnie and that they
haven't been married at court, which I was afraid might
happen. We'll delay the wedding as long as it's possible.
Tell him, if he loves her he must come for her there. Soon.
Do you understand me? Can you remember all that?" She
stared intently into the boy's face and saw him nod vigor-
ously.

"I'll tell him, Marjorie, don't worry. I will get it right."
He tucked the letter into his doublet, his chin set with
determination.

Then suddenly he tensed, glancing over his shoulder.
Someone was coming down the passage, whistling. With a
quick smile and a nod he ducked out of sight behind a
door, leaving Marjorie alone.

"Did you get the letter to him safely?" Isabel asked at once
when Marjorie returned to her room.

Marjorie nodded. "I gave it to him, my lady, and I've
sworn him to secrecy, never fear."

Isabel had slipped off her head-dress and was slowly
unplaiting her braids. She reached wearily for the brush.
"You know," she said with a bitter little laugh, "I think
Ian was happy here. The king doesn't seem to be an unjust
man at all."

"No, my lady. It was your father who was unhappy."
Marjorie's voice was strangely gentle. She took the brush
from Isabel's hand and began to brush her hair with long
firm strokes.

There was a flicker of light in the darkness beyond the
open window and both girls looked up, startled, in time to
see another zigzag flash of eldritch green over the distant
mountains.

"Lightning in the hills." Isabel laughed uneasily.
"That's an ill omen, I think." She shivered as, slowly, the
rain began to patter down onto the sill, blackening the
stone, slanting through the deep embrasure to fall on the

sweet hay which covered the floor. "But if it rains hard we won't be able to travel tomorrow," she added and glanced round hopefully. "Pray for it to rain, Marjorie. Pray for it to rain. Hard."

CHAPTER
THREE

IT did not rain hard enough, however, and Sir Duncan's horses were ready soon after dawn the next day. Isabel, her throat tight with misery, clung for a moment to her father and her brother, who had come to see them off in the raw early light which filtered down between the high walls into the dim courtyard of the palace, then she turned unwillingly to face Sir Duncan.

He had abandoned his ceremonial court gown of the day before for a short fur-trimmed tunic worn over a shirt and leather doublet and long buskins; and he carried a long sword at his belt. Unlike his men, he wore no armour of any kind. Reluctantly she glanced up at his face. His dark aquiline features were set in a grim mask as he stepped to her side and held out his hand to help her mount.

Why, he hates the idea of this marriage as much as I do, she thought, trying to read the carefully hidden expression in his eyes as she allowed him to throw her up on to her grey mare.

For a moment he remained at her side, staring up at her face. She hastily looked away, but not before she had seen with a little stab of surprise how strangely attractive he could be when the mask was lifted – only for a second – to betray the hint of a smile. Then it had slipped down again and she found herself staring, puzzled, into eyes as hard as agate. The next moment he had turned away and she was left sitting there desolately, hugging herself into the bleak warmth of her cloak against the cold, not letting herself glance back to where her father stood, his arm round the boy's shoulders, waiting.

Sir Duncan swung himself up on to the back of his own great black stallion and riding to the head of his men raised his arm to signal their departure. In a moment they were through the archway and out of sight of the small group of watching figures.

They rode fast down the muddy tracks towards the south-east, the cantering horses sending great clods of earth flying high into the air behind them as the mellow autumn sun began to dispel the clinging mists.

Sir Duncan rode at the head of his men, and never once on their journey did he glance back at the two women in the centre of the tightly-grouped escort. Beside him the standard-bearer carried aloft his banner – the sable fox of Glencarnie with its grinning bloody jaws, hunting across a field of rippling gold; the same creature was blazoned on the tabards of his men and from it he had derived his nickname, one which suited him ideally, Isabel thought with a little shiver of apprehension.

In spite of herself, she could not resist glancing from time to time at the broad shoulders of the man who, the king had decreed, was to be her husband. There was something indefinably fascinating about the arrogant set of his head and the careless way he sat the great snorting destrier as he rode beneath the black and gold of his banner, and she could not put out of her mind the strangely attractive half-smile he had given her as he looked up at her before they set off.

Afterwards she remembered very little of the journey to Glencarnie itself. It took them several hours, riding through the wild lowland hills, with a short break at midday to rest the horses and take some food. The sun was still up, mistily red above the rim of the mountains when at last they drew near the lonely castle, high on its crags over the river Carnie, and began the long, hard canter up to it. Half-way up the hill Sir Duncan raised his hand, bringing the horsemen to a rearing halt. Wheeling, he rode back and spoke to her for the first time on the journey.

"Well, my lady, we have reached our destination."

Isabel was holding herself very straight in the saddle, determined he should not see the sudden wave of despair and loneliness which overtook her at his words.

Instead of looking at him as his horse fell in step beside

hers she raised her eyes to the sprawl of grey towers and walls above them and in spite of herself she caught her breath. Glencarnie was far larger than her father's castle. From where they approached it, its position seemed impregnable and she could not help being grudgingly impressed.

The track they were following skirted the shoulder of the hill to avoid the steep cliffs which overhung the river beneath the high northern walls of the castle and then it plunged into a thick wood. When they emerged from the trees there was a bare strip of cleared ground in front of them and beyond it they could see the castle itself, the bridge over the moat leading under a high shadowy arch. Beyond the arch Isabel glimpsed a group of waiting figures.

"We are expected, it seems." Sir Duncan glanced sideways at her, reining back his black horse to keep pace with her tired mare. "No doubt some over-busy messenger has brought the news ahead of us that the Black Fox is bringing a bride to Glencarnie. A pity; I would have given a lot to see my mother's face when she first heard the news." Again that forbidding smile, without warmth. "She will not, I suspect, be quite as pleased as I am to have the daughter of Strathblair under her roof."

"In that she and I will be in complete agreement, Sir Duncan," Isabel retorted gamely. She looked at him squarely, wondering how she had seen anything even remotely attractive in the man's smile. "The idea of living beneath your roof sickens me."

His brown eyes hardened. "You would rather be dead, no doubt, madam."

There was no disguising the sudden threat in his voice and she gasped, biting back the words of retort which had been on her lips. She looked down at her hands, blushing uncomfortably beneath her hood, as at her side she heard a quiet mirthless laugh.

He urged his mount into a canter and rode again to the head of his men to lead the column of horses across the high bridge and under the archway with its iron-toothed portcullis poised menacingly above their heads. The inner close, surrounded by high grey stone walls, was deep in shadow and very cold, but Isabel forgot her tiredness and the gloom of her surroundings as she saw with foreboding the group of people who were waiting amidst the milling horsemen.

Sir Duncan swung himself from his horse and appeared suddenly at her stirrup, his hands raised to help her down. Behind him at the forefront of the reception group, a few paces away, stood a tall elderly woman, ramrod straight in her fur-trimmed cloak. Her dark face and hard brown eyes were so like those of her son that there was no mistaking her identity.

Isabel found her hand in Duncan's before she realised it and had no alternative but to allow him to lift her to the ground. Once there she tried to free herself from his grip, but he held her wrist effortlessly.

"Mother, may I present the lady our king has chosen to be my wife: Lady Isabel Douglass of Strathblair."

Isabel curtseyed, her eyes on the woman's face. It had grown ugly with dislike and at the sight she heard Marjorie, who had slid unaided from her horse close behind her, give an involuntary gasp of fear.

"So. King James thinks to end generations of war between our families with an exchange of rings." The deep clipped voice was heavy with sarcasm. "I am astonished, Duncan, that the Black Fox should allow himself to be bought off with a milksop. What hold, pray, does the king have over you, to make you accept this . . ." she hesitated, her lips forming themselves into an elegant sneer, "this creature?"

Isabel caught her breath. Hostility she had expected, but open hatred such as this? She took a step back, clutching her heavy travelling cloak around her defensively, and was brought up short as Duncan put his arm around her shoulders. He gripped her fast, pushing her forward until she found herself unwillingly face to face with the other woman.

"My lady mother, Isabel, has not had time to grow used to the idea of our betrothal." Duncan's voice in her ear was tightly controlled. "When she has, I know she will give you the welcome you should expect to receive from the Lady of Glencarnie and kiss you as her daughter."

Mother and son glared at each other across her for a moment – both tall, both proud and both very angry. Then the old woman gave way with a slight inclination of the head.

"My son sees fit to rebuke me, my lady. It appears that I have forgotten the sacred duties of hospitality, which are due to any traveller – however unwelcome." She shot a venomous look at her son and there was still more than a trace of irony in her voice as she went on. "You will certainly be tired after your long ride. My girl Marie will show you to your chamber." Unsmilingly she beckoned forward one of the women from the crowd of staring onlookers behind her. "Take the lady from Strathblair and her maid to the guest chamber in the Drum Tower. I take it," she added, glancing superciliously at her son, "that you wish the lady to have the best guest chamber?"

"Naturally, Mother, until she shares mine." He bowed slightly, his hand still gripping Isabel's shoulder.

She felt a little tingle of fear run down her spine at his words, but she held herself straight and forced herself to smile. "Thank you, Lady Crawfurd. I should indeed be glad to rest after the ride."

This time she found it easier to disengage herself from Duncan's grip and, her head held high, she followed Marie, with Marjorie close on her heels, away from the silent, curious faces, across the cold courtyard and into a door at the foot of a great circular tower at the northern end of the castle. No one made a move to follow them.

The staircase was quite dark save for the light of a tallow candle which burned in a bracket just inside the door. Seizing it, Marie set off upwards, not looking round to see if they were following.

Stumbling on the unfamiliar uneven steps Isabel went after her, with Marjorie so close behind that once or twice the girl stepped on her train in her effort not to be left alone in the dark. Marie stopped at the second door they came to and flung it open. The chamber inside was dark and cold and cavernous. No one had even lighted a fire.

Isabel had to fight back her tears as she looked into the echoing circular room. Unconsciously she held her hand out towards her maid for reassurance and Marjorie gripped it hard. The two girls clung together as Marie walked unsmilingly to a heavy table with her candle. The unsteady flame revealed two taper holders standing side by side on the dusty oak surface. As she lit the tapers the pale lights flared to reveal a large curtained bed, a few stools and a table. That was all. The deep embrasured windows were shuttered but the bare walls had no hangings and the floor itself was of flagstones, white with draught-borne wood ash from the hearth.

Looking round in amazement Marjorie suddenly found her voice. "Well, if this is the kind of hospitality you find south of the Forth, I'd rather choose to cross the Pentland Firth and live in the land of the Norsemen any day!" She released Isabel's hand and ran to pick up one of the branches of tapers, holding it high till the shadows ran and flickered over the high vaulted ceiling. "Holy Virgin! Do they expect you to sleep here?" She felt the bed covers and then wiped her hand with a shudder against her cloak. "The bedding is damp for a start. You'd die of a rheum in the lungs before you ever got to Sir Duncan's bed, that's for sure."

"Hush, Marjie!" Isabel glanced over her shoulder nervously at their escort. She turned to the woman, who was waiting, her face impassive, by the table. "Can you see the fire is lighted for us, and bring us some hot water, Marie? We've had a long ride." She had almost started to unfasten her cloak, but then she thought better of it, pulling it more closely round her instead.

"And have them bring floor coverings, and more screens for the windows while you're at it," Marjorie went on tartly. She pulled the heavy covers off the bed with an effort and tumbled them to the floor. "And we'll need fresh linen and rugs for the bed. These feel as though they've been down a well for ten years!"

Isabel sank down on one of the stools and gazed miserably at the empty hearth. Her head had begun to throb with exhaustion and nerves and she was shivering uncontrollably. "Will they bring our chests up soon? I've a fur wrap somewhere and a spare mantle . . ."

She broke off at a sudden movement in the doorway behind them.

Sir Duncan was standing in the shadows, surveying the room.

"It appears that though my mother was expecting you, she forgot to prepare your rooms," he commented drily. "I regret that. I did not look for such a lack of readiness, I assure you."

Before Isabel had time to reply he had stepped back on to the stairway and they heard him shout down the echoing steps in a voice which was meant to be obeyed without delay. His summons was answered at once by two panting squires, attired in the Glencarnie livery.

"Fire, lights, strewing herbs, linen, quickly!" he snapped. "I want this room made fit for a queen."

The squires scurried away as two of Duncan's men-at-arms appeared in the doorway carrying the first of Isabel's heavy coffers, and with five or six men and three maid-servants hurrying round the room, it did not take long for it to be transformed from echoing emptiness to something approaching comfort.

All the time the logs were being carried up and lit and the bed made ready, Isabel sat mutely on her stool, while Marjorie scurried round giving orders, seeing that their belongings were stowed in the right places. Both young women were acutely conscious the whole time of Duncan standing silently watching the proceedings from the doorway, arms folded, but only when the last servant had run, bowing, from the room did he step forward at last.

He walked up to Isabel and calmly putting his fingers beneath her chin forced her face up to look at his. He surveyed her gravely for a moment, then, unexpectedly, his grim features broke into a smile. She felt her heart give an uncomfortable lurch at the sight. This was indeed a man any woman might find dangerously attractive when the cold mask, which she feared he was going to keep exclusively for her, was gone.

"You look exhausted, sweetheart." His voice was silky.

"So I'll spare you the ordeal of supper in my great hall
tonight. I'll have food brought to you here."

Relief flooded through her. She had been dreading
another confrontation with Lady Crawfurd – or with any
of his household, tired and depressed as she was, and the
longer she could put off the moment of her first public
appearance the happier she would be.

She shrank away from Duncan's hand, but his fingers
were still there, beneath her chin, forcing her face up
towards his. He stooped. Before she realised what he was
doing he had kissed her lightly upon the lips, then releasing her abruptly he stepped away from her and was gone.
Both girls listened as his footsteps echoed down the winding stairs. Then Marjorie ran to the door and closing it
after him she shot the bolt home. She leaned against it with
a sigh of relief. "I'll open it again for nothing but food.
Nothing!" she cried.

She glanced at Isabel. The girl's face was flaming as she
pressed her fingers to her cheeks, and Marjorie frowned.
Then calmly she went to her mistress's side. "I'll help you
with your head-dress, my lady, and brush your hair for
you, shall I? Then I'll find your bed-gown. The sooner
you're in bed with that hot brick at your feet the happier I
shall be."

But even when at last she was warm beneath the fur
rugs, propped against feather pillows with the loose gown
draped around her bare shoulders, the two spots of scarlet
remained on Isabel's cheeks. Her heart was beating painfully as each time she thought of Duncan a strange excitement stirred in her. Furiously she tried to drive it away.
He deserved nothing but contempt for his treatment of her
so far, and contempt was what she intended to show him.

When someone knocked at the door she jumped nervously, but it was only the food as he had promised. Two
pages entered when Marjorie drew the bolt, carrying trays
laden with bowls of spicy stew and bread and pasties and a
jug of wine.

"I don't think I can eat anything, Marjie," Isabel commented doubtfully as the other girl brought her a bowl and
a spoon.

"You will. Come on, it's near enough cold already after coming from the kitchens, and the lord only knows how far away they are in this great place." Marjorie put the spoon in her fingers. "Come on," she coaxed, "eat. While I put the wine by the fire to mull."

To her surprise when she tasted the food Isabel found she was hungry after all, and she and Marjorie between them managed to eat a good meal. Then she lay back comfortably against the pillows, drawing her knees up under the covers. The excitement had gone, and in its place she felt a terrible aching weariness.

"When do you think he means to . . . marry me?" she hesitated slightly, almost unable to bring herself to say the words.

Marjorie pulled a face. "Soon, I fear. I think he means to do it soon. But you've got to delay it as long as possible."

She had not told Isabel of her message to Andrew. So much might go wrong. The boy might not deliver the message to him, or he might get it back to front; Andrew might have left Strathblair already, that same day, and be anywhere by now – already at court, or worse still on his way back to France, or unbelievably he might not want to come. She pushed aside the last possibility, but even so she did not want to raise Isabel's hopes. Not yet. She glanced at the girl's pinched face as she lay back in the bed, and wondered whether a ray of hope might be what she needed to sustain her over the coming weeks – or days. She refused to think that it might be only a matter of days.

"How can we delay it, Marjie?" Isabel closed her eyes against the firelight. "The king expects us to marry at once."

"We'll think of something." Marjorie was stacking the pewter bowls back on the tray. Absent-mindedly she helped herself to a piece of left-over pasty and began to chew it. "You can always pretend to be ill, of course, at the last moment. Or you could say your horoscope was not propitious."

Isabel laughed mirthlessly from her pillow. "I can't see

Sir Duncan postponing the wedding because my star is not in the ascendant!"

"Well, something else then," Marjorie pushed the tray away irritably to the far side of the table. "Anything to hold him off a while longer. I know. You could say you had sworn an oath before the Blessed Virgin that you too would remain a virgin, until your next birthday."

Isabel could not keep back a smile. "Or my thirtieth, or my fortieth perhaps? I feel somehow that he would find a way of releasing me from my vow before the week was out. But we must try and think of something, Marjie. He –" she hesitated. "He scares me so much."

Marjorie refilled a goblet with the warmed wine and brought it to the bed. She nodded soberly. "Aye, my lady," she admitted quietly. "He scares me too."

The next morning they were awakened early by the chapel bell. Isabel slipped from the warm bed which she and Marjorie had shared and pulling on the bed-gown ran barefoot to the window near her. Unbarring the rough shutters she leaned out as far as she could. The window overlooked the cobbled bailey at the heart of the castle, and at the far end she could see the turret with the swinging bell which marked the chapel. Below, people were running across the close from every side in answer to its summons. She shivered. It was an icy morning and the sun had not not yet risen above the surrounding hills.

"Will you go to hear Mass, my lady?" Marjorie was sitting up in bed, watching her. Isabel pushed the shutter back across the window.

"Not today. I don't want to meet them all till I have to." She watched as Marjorie, dragging on her robe, gingerly set her feet to the cold heather-covered flags and ran to the fireplace. She threw on fresh logs and stirred the white ashes into sparks beneath them, then she set fresh tapers and lit them to give them better light to dress by.

They were barely ready when there was an imperious knocking at the door. Marjorie ran to open it and stepped back with an exclamation and a small curtsey. Lady Crawfurd stood outside, immaculately neat in a veil and wimple and a gown of indigo velvet. She was alone. Gesturing to Marjorie to close the door she walked across to the stool near the fire and seated herself. Isabel was standing at the table, her hairbrush in her hand, her long dark hair still lying loose on her shoulders.

There was a moment of silence as Isabel exchanged frightened glances with her maid. She took a deep breath. "Good morning, Lady Crawfurd." It was hard to smile at the woman whose face was like carved brown stone, but she forced herself to do it.

"I expect my household and –" a slight hesitation, "– my guests, to attend chapel every morning," the old lady stated, her hands folded in her lap. "I trust that tomorrow you will feel able to join us."

Isabel opened her mouth to retort, then she saw Marjorie's eyes fixed humbly on the ground and she had second thoughts. "I'm sorry, ma'am," she said meekly. "The ride must have been more tiring than I realised."

"No doubt!" The woman had a way of snapping her lips shut after each sentence, like a trap closing. Isabel shivered.

Lady Crawfurd noticed at once and a strange gleam came into her eye. Her cheeks puckered momentarily as she considered her words, then, looking straight ahead of her into the fire, she said, "You should know that I have no intention of allowing my son to proceed with this marriage. It is out of the question." Again her lips snapped shut.

Isabel swallowed, her heart beginning to pound irregularly as she listened. Could it be that this formidable woman was offering her a way out of her predicament?

"It would please me greatly, ma'am, if you could find a means to avoid the marriage. You should know that I am as opposed to it as you are." She hesitated as the old lady's eyebrows shot up. Then she rushed on, "Only the king himself could force me to marry your son. If it hadn't been for my brother I should have refused absolutely. I would rather have entered a convent."

"Indeed." Lady Crawfurd rose to her feet and stood for a moment looking down at her. "Your views, child, are of no importance. It would have been an unheard-of piece of luck for you to marry into the house of Glencarnie, but for us – for us, it would have meant total *dishonour*."

She hissed the last word so suddenly that Isabel drew back, startled. The old woman with her white veil and wimple had looked suddenly with her great hooded eyes like a snake about to strike. "How we can avoid this marriage, I have not yet decided," Lady Crawfurd went on, lowering her voice. "It seems to me there may be only one way out of it . . ."

After a significant pause she gave an enigmatic smile and then with slow stately steps she turned and waving Marjorie away from the door she left the room.

Isabel sat down on the bed. Her legs were shaking suddenly. "What did she mean?" she asked at last.

Marjorie shrugged. "Dreadful old witch. I should think her husband dropped dead the first night he lay with her!"

Isabel giggled nervously. Then she looked serious. "No, her husband died on the battlefield, at the hand of a Strathblair. She will never forget that, Marjie, or forgive. I think she meant . . ." She paused, stroking with agitated fingers the fur rug on which she was sitting. "Well, I think she meant it as a threat." She glanced up at her maid. "I've got to find a way out of here, Marjie. I've got to. The king can't have realised how strongly they all felt, how much they hate me here."

"My lady, there is something I must tell you." Marjorie had made up her mind quite suddenly. She ran to the door and listened intently, then, satisfied that there was no one there, she came and knelt at Isabel's feet. "Listen," she whispered. "I hadn't meant to say anything yet, in case he couldn't come for some reason, but I think you should know. I sent a message back with Lord Ian. That your Andrew should come and fetch you somehow before it's too late." She looked up at Isabel's face anxiously.

For a moment her mistress sat gazing at her in disbelief, then suddenly her face was bright with hope.

"When did you send him a message? And how?"

"The night before last, my lady. With your letter to him."

"But my letter told him not to think of me any more." Isabel jumped up in agitation and pushing past Marjorie ran to the window on the far side of the room which looked out towards the north.

Their tower stood on that side of the castle on the top of the cliffs which dropped dizzily down towards the river hundreds of feet below. Glancing down she drew back, her head reeling at the drop below her. "Andrew won't come. He can't. He'll think of his duty to my father or to the king."

"He'll think of his love for you, my lady, if he's any kind of a man at all." Scrambling to her feet Marjorie came close to her. "He loves you. He'll come. He would die to save you, I know he –" She broke off suddenly as they both heard distinctly the sound of a step somewhere outside the door to the room.

Putting her fingers to her lips warningly Marjorie rose and ran silently towards it, grabbing hold of the heavy ring handle and quickly wrenching it open.

Outside stood a tall, pale-faced young man wearing a short heavily-embroidered ornamental gown and skin-tight dark green hose. He seemed taken aback for a moment as the door was flung open in his face, but he recovered himself almost at once. His gaze went past Marjorie to where a white-faced Isabel was standing in the middle of the room. He bowed stiffly and she noticed at once a slight lift of the eyebrow as he took in her undressed hair.

"My lady." There was a pause as he stared round the room.

"What is it?" Isabel asked sharply. She didn't like the way his glance kept coming back to her, running over her, noting every detail of her dress, seeming to see right through it to her shift and even beyond.

He smiled. There was, she decided, more than a touch of insolence in his manner.

"Sir Duncan wants you to join him, my lady," he said at last. "He feels that you are perhaps shy of coming and finding your way around by yourself and he is very anxious," his eyes flickered momentarily to Marjorie who was standing beside him, "that you should not get lost."

"It's good of him to send you." Isabel clenched her teeth. "Perhaps you'd be good enough to wait outside? Then my maid can finish my hair and we will join you."

She wondered for a moment, as he hesitated, if he were going to refuse, but he thought better of it, obviously, and bowing again he withdrew from the room.

The two women looked at each other uneasily. "Do you think he heard what we were saying?" Marjorie murmured after she had shut the door behind him. She took up Isabel's brush. "This place is probably full of spies. We'll have to take such care, my lady."

Isabel swallowed. "We'll take care. And we'll get away. Somehow we'll have to get away, Marjie, we must."

With her cloak well wrapped round her Isabel led the way out of the door and down the long winding stairs of the Drum Tower. The young man was waiting for them at the outside door, leaning negligently against the wall, a straw between his teeth. He let it fall from his mouth as he saw her and languidly straightening up he led the way out into the cold misty morning. The bailey was deserted as far as Isabel could see as she followed him past the long range of stables with Marjorie close on her heels.

He paused at the door to the great hall and flung it open, bowing Isabel past him, and she caught sight of the look of insolence in his eyes again as she walked in. Then she stopped. Marjorie had let out a startled exclamation close behind her. The man had put out his arm, barring the maid's way.

"Not you," he said.

"What do you mean?" Marjorie rounded on him. "I stay with my mistress." She began to push ineffectually against him.

"Let her pass," Isabel commanded. "She's my personal maid. She goes everywhere with me."

"Not here, lady." His arm still rested like a bar between them, his hand almost casually clasping the opposite door jamb. "The Black Fox wishes to view his bride. Alone." He smiled.

Isabel was furious. "You let her pass," she said.

The man didn't move. He grinned more widely still as Marjorie took hold of his arm and tried to drag it out of her way, his eyes all the time fixed insolently on Isabel's face.

"I said, let her pass," she repeated, trying to keep her voice steady. She glanced round for help, but the high-ceilinged great hall with its smoky rafters appeared to be empty.

She longed to bring her fist hard into the broadly grinning mouth – anything to stop that insolent leer. But then, as she was watching his face, it disappeared abruptly. In its place a look of surprise and anguish flashed across the man's features. Marjorie, taking advantage of his preoccupation with her mistress, had sunk her teeth into his forearm through the thin material of his doublet. The man let out a howl of pain and abruptly lowered his hand.

Behind them there was a quiet laugh. All three stood rigid. Then, slowly turning round to face the sound she had already come to dread, Isabel could feel her throat contricting with fear as the tall dark figure of Duncan Crawfurd appeared from the shadows behind a screen.

"One up to the ladies, I think, Murdoch," he chuckled. "You undoubtedly got the worst of that encounter. Oh, come on, man, I'll wager the skin is not even broken."

The young man's face had gone white and then scarlet, as sheepishly he rubbed his arm.

"And in future," Duncan's voice hardened suddenly, "you will obey the commands of my Lady Isabel, do you understand? Now, go."

Murdoch nodded without speaking, but as he turned to leave Isabel saw the venomous look he flashed at her.

"And now, my lady," Duncan went on when he had gone. "Will you please ask your woman to leave us? That young man's methods may be ill-considered, but his message was accurate. I wish to talk with you. Alone."

He turned and strode to the end of the hall and stood, obviously waiting for her, gazing down at the enormous fire which burned in the hearth there.

Isabel licked her lips nervously. "You'd better go, Marjie." she murmured under her breath.

She walked slowly down the long hall after him and stopped a little behind him, her head held high.

"You wished to speak to me, sir?"

He turned. The fire reflected strange shadows on the strong features of his face as he stood looking at her, and she felt herself quail beneath the intensity of his gaze. Unconsciously she straightened her shoulders.

For a moment she thought he wasn't going to speak at all, then he took a step towards her. It brought him very close.

"We have various things to discuss. The date of our marriage for one. I suggest we choose St Matthew's Day. There seems very little point in delaying the ceremony."

Isabel thought quickly. "Surely that's not long enough? Your mother would object, I know, and . . ."

"My mother will object whatever date I set. Ten days or ten years. It will make no difference."

She was very conscious of how near to her he was standing.

"Do you have other objections to the date – of your own?" he asked. There was a trace of a smile somewhere at the corners of his eyes. Abruptly she looked down, staring hard at the intricate silver-worked buckle on his belt. "Of course not. But a few days only – well," she shrugged. "It scarcely gives me time to prepare a bride-chest. My father only told me, as you know, the day before I left Strathblair that I was to marry, and I had no chance to order my women to make me any new gowns. I should feel very bad, coming to my wedding with nothing to . . ." She hesitated, catching sight of the expression on his face.

"Nothing to wear?" His voice was mocking. Cautiously she glanced up under her eyelashes. His face was completely impassive again at once, but she noticed suddenly that there were warm gold glints in the brown of his eyes. He was laughing at her.

"It may be a joke for a man, sir," she said with all the dignity she could gather, "but for a woman it is important."

"For the priest too, my sweet, should you come to take your vows naked!"

She stepped back, blushing. He had not taken his eyes from her face and although his expression was still unsmiling she could see he was determined to tease her. She felt her anger and indignation rising.

"How long would it take you to prepare this vast array, my lady?" he went on innocently. "With the help of every sewing maid at Glencarnie, do you think six months would do it?"

"Oh yes, easily," she began with a quick surge of relief. Then she saw the open laughter on his face and her heart sank. "You are making fun of me, Sir Duncan," she said angrily. "But if your maids are even half as good as those at Strathblair, they might be ready in that time.   You wouldn't want me to look like a beggar in rags when I'm Lady of Glencarnie."

Her eyes flashed with fury as he greeted her statement with a shout of laughter.

"You would be beautiful even in rags, madam. But as it happens the maids of Glencarnie are ten times quicker than yours, and so it will take them but a week. So –" he looked down at her, his face suddenly serious again, "we have the date fixed. Now, about your own maid. I shall give you tiring women and maids. You will have no further need of her, so you can send her away."

There was a moment of shocked silence. Isabel gasped. "But Marjorie is my companion. You can't send her away."

"I think I must. She is altogether too much above herself. I do not allow disobedient servants in my house."

"She is not disobedient to me!" Isabel replied hotly. "She is loyal and kind, and besides she is my friend."

She could have bitten out her tongue as she saw him raise one eyebrow in surprised disdain. "The future Lady of Glencarnie, madam, does not have maids for friends," he said acidly.

"Maybe Ladies of Glencarnie don't," she retorted, her fury rising in her panic at the thought of being without Marjorie, "but may I point out, Sir Duncan that I am the daughter of an earl, and that I do!"

"Had you not been the daughter of an earl, I should not

have found you good enough to be my wife, Isabel." His voice was suddenly dangerously quiet. "You will obey me in this. The girl goes. And today."

Isabel clenched her fists. "If she goes, I go." She was trembling with anger, unconscious of the futility of such a threat.

He smiled coldly, and at the sight this time she felt another tingle of fear. There was no humour in his face. "You will never go without my permission, Isabel. Glen-carnie is your home now, and will be as long as you live."

There was a long pause. Desperately she tried to control her anger and her rising panic. She had to try and make him understand. Forcing herself somehow to be calm, she glanced up at him. "If it is to be truly my home, sir, I am sure you wouldn't deprive me of the only companion I have amongst a household of strangers, and besides," she added on sudden inspiration, "she sews exceptionally well. Her embroidery is famous throughout the king-dom."

He laughed quietly. "Ah, so there is one thing at last in her favour. Well, perhaps in that case I might allow her to stay – until our marriage only. Once the sewing is finished, then she must go. Agreed?"

She breathed a quick sigh of relief. It was a respite at least. "She will, Sir Duncan. And I will keep her out of your sight, sewing in my apartments, till then."

A log had slipped in the hearth behind him and a curtain of flame shot up suddenly as the dry bark crackled and flared. The hall was full of the scent of bitter smoke. He took a step towards her and reached out to take her by the shoulders. "We should do very well together, you and I, once you have learned the meek obedience required of a wife." He looked down into her eyes. She tried to step back but he held her tightly, his fingers biting suddenly into her flesh. "Tell me, Isabel, did you have any lovers before me?"

His eyes held hers, and she could feel her mouth going dry. His clothes smelt of leather and musk and sandal-wood. Her head began to reel.

"Naturally," she managed to sound defiant.

"And did they kiss you, Isabel?" he went on quietly. His face was very near to hers.

She started to struggle, a lump forming suddenly in her throat as she thought with piercing longing of her gentle Andrew. "He was worth a hundred of you, Duncan Craw-furd, a hundred!" she cried out desperately, pulling away from him, pushing at him helplessly as he drew her close against his chest. His arm behind her shoulders was like a bar of iron. She felt it snatching her veil and the filmy material slipped from the fillet on her hair, dislodging the heavy braids which tumbled down to her shoulders.

His face was only inches from hers as he held her against him. Again the gold lights flickered in his eyes. "Did he have a name, this lover of yours?" he murmured.

"I won't ever tell you that," she gasped. She raised her hand to try once more to push him away but he caught her wrist with ease. And then his lips were on hers.

As she struggled she was conscious suddenly once again of the surge of strange wild excitement coursing through her veins as his mouth burned against hers, and for a moment she felt herself lie limply in his arms, shaken by its violence. His grip tightened triumphantly and at once she began again to struggle, fury and terror driving out the peculiar unwanted elation. With a wrench she tore her arm free and brought her nails up towards his face, but his hand caught hers, imprisoning it, and he laughed softly as he kissed her again. What would have happened next she could only guess as his love-making was interrupted sud-denly by a blood-curdling scream from the far end of the hall.

"Glencarnie!"

The name rose and hung like an echo in the blackened rafters above them for a full minute before he released her and pushed her abruptly away.

He swung round with an oath and Isabel staggered away from him, her senses still spinning. She put her hand to her bruised mouth and found blood on her fingers. Her cheeks were burning and her heart was hammering pain-fully somewhere below her ribs. She stared, half-dazed, at the distant corner of the hall from where the scream had come, but it was blocked by screens and she could see no one.

In a few strides Duncan was there, pulling them aside, hurling them back against the wall to reveal a service door out towards the castle kitchens. There was no one to be seen. He turned back, his face grim. "Go to your room," he called abruptly, and he swung round again, ducking out of sight through the door, leaving her alone in the hall.

Trembling, Isabel stooped to pick up her torn and trampled veil. Then she turned and ran out of the deserted hall into the misty sunlight of the great bailey court.

Her chamber in the Drum Tower was empty. There was no sign anywhere of Marjorie as with a stifled sob she flung herself down on the bed, feeling still, on her mouth, the fierce imprint of his lips.

A narrow beam of sunlight reached down through the deep embrasure of one of the windows, falling across the bed and warming her a little as she lay there unmoving. It was a long time before she stirred, but then a small sound in the doorway across the room made her sit up, pushing the hair of her loosened, tangled braids out of her eyes.

"Is that you, Marjie?" she called with relief. "Come here. Help me . ." She broke off as she glanced towards the doorway. A woman was standing there, tall and slim and very beautiful, her gown of deep green velvet exactly reflecting the green of her eyes. She waited a moment in complete silence, watching, as Isabel dragged herself to her feet. Then at last she spoke.

"So, this is the lady the Black Fox has brought back to Glencarnie." Her deep melodious voice was throbbing with sarcasm. "His little present from the king." She took a step into the room, her heavy skirts rustling in the deep heather, and involuntarily Isabel took a step back. A warning pulse had begun to beat somewhere in her throat.

"Do you really think he would marry you?" the woman went on quietly. The ray of sunshine caught the copper fillet on her veil and the chestnut lights in her hair which lay unbraided on her shoulders beneath it. Her finely-cut lips twisted into a smile. "Do you really imagine that a Crawfurd of Glencarnie would do *anything* to please King Jamie?"

Isabel swallowed and tried to regain some composure before the cool gaze of this strange woman. "I'm sorry," she stammered, trying to keep her voice level. "I don't understand. What has all this to do with you?"

The woman smiled again. She had beautiful white even teeth. "It has everything to do with me, child. I am Margaret Stewart."

She paused as if waiting for a reaction, and when Isabel continued to look puzzled she went on impatiently, "I am the woman with whom the Black Fox shares his plate at table, and his bed at night." She stopped triumphantly.

Isabel gasped.

"And I am the woman he intends to marry. Make no mistake about that. No one, not even our well-beloved king, will set up anyone in my place at Glencarnie." She took another step forward and it carried her out of the sunlight and into deep shadow.

Isabel automatically moved back. Half of her was immensely relieved at the news that Duncan already had a woman; after all it was hardly surprising, but to her amazement the other half of her was numb with shock. She had felt a pang of something which seemed very close to jealousy at Margaret's words, and she was furious with herself. They deserved each other, this tempestuous-looking woman and Duncan Crawfurd.

"I had no idea Sir Duncan was already betrothed, Lady Margaret," she said as haughtily as she could. "He did not see fit to enlighten me on the fact. But believe me, it was not my idea to come here. I would go at once if I could. I'm sure Sir Duncan must be as appalled as I am –" She thought suddenly of his passionate kiss in the great hall and her cheeks coloured violently. His behaviour there did not seem to support her argument at all.

Margaret obviously thought so too. "Oh yes, I saw you two together there just now," she sneered. "I even called out before I could stop myself. He's always amused himself with women; he can't keep his hands off them, and he'd make mincemeat of a child like you. But marry you? Never."

She took another step forward and Isabel, retreating, found herself brought up short by a large coffer standing against the wall. She clenched her fists nervously in the folds of her skirt. Suddenly she was very afraid of Margaret Stewart.

"Lady Margaret, I assure you that this marriage is quite abhorrent to me. I should give anything to get out of it. Really . . ." She broke off. The other woman was moving again. Isabel could see the details of the gold and pearl filigree necklace at her throat now as she came closer.

"I intend to see, my dear, that the marriage is also abhorrent to Duncan," she murmured quietly.

Isabel tried to stifle her rising panic. She side-stepped away from the coffer and found herself trapped between it and the curve of the wall. Margaret was only a few feet from her now.

"Duncan has a horror of ugly women, my dear," she murmured again, smiling sweetly. "Only a few months ago he dangled after a serving wench here. He even got her with child." Her eyes were narrow slits now. "But then she had an unfortunate accident. Her face got badly burned, you see; very badly burned. He never looked at her after that . . ."

Isabel watched, paralysed, as Margaret reached quietly into the embroidered purse which swung from her girdle. Fascinated, she followed every movement with her eyes, not daring to breathe. Then her heart seemed to stop beating altogether. Glinting wickedly between the other woman's fingers there was a small jewelled dirk.

CHAPTER
FOUR

SHE never knew how long she stood there, mesmerized by the shining blade, before suddenly she came to life again. She lunged at Margaret's hand, grabbing at the woman's wrist, trying desperately to shake the dagger from her grasp. Margaret was surprisingly strong. With seemingly little effort, she held on to the dirk and slowly, despite all Isabel's efforts, she raised her hand, the blade menacingly angled between them.

And then suddenly it was all over. There was a furious exclamation from the doorway. With three long strides Duncan was across the room and behind Margaret, wresting the dirk from her fingers with a vicious twist of her hand before he flung her away. She fell to her knees on the floor by the bed, weeping and cursing.

"Stupid bitch!" He hurled the words after her, and then he turned to Isabel and gently ran his hands over her pale face. "Are you hurt?" he asked quietly.

She shook her head numbly. Shocked as she was, she could still hear Margaret's bitter words ringing in her mind: "Duncan has a horror of ugly women . . ." And he had proved it true, for here he was, before anything else, running his fingers across her face to check that she was unscarred. She pulled away from him abruptly, nauseated.

"No, Sir Duncan, I'm not marked, have no fear on that score." Her voice was cold. She turned to look at Margaret, who was still lying sobbing angrily among the strewn heather. "Perhaps you had better help the Lady Margaret to her feet." She ignored him and went to the window, grateful to feel the cold wind on her flushed face. She gazed, unseeing, across the river towards the distant hills.

She waited tensely, half expecting to feel his hands again on her shoulders. She refused to let herself look round as she heard the sounds of the other woman rising to her feet and brushing the loose heather stems from her gown.

"Get back to your rooms, Margaret," she heard his voice, low and intimate, caressing. "This girl doesn't concern you. Don't be foolish. I'll come to you later."

A minute later the door banged. There was a pause and then she heard his voice, directly behind her.

"I guessed she would come straight up here. Thank God, I got to you in time. Are you sure you are unharmed?" As she didn't move or reply he went on, "You mustn't be frightened by Margaret. She won't try and injure you again, you know."

It was then she turned to face him. He was holding the dirk in his hand; she could see the gems sparkling in the cross-set handle.

"I didn't know, Sir Duncan, that someone else had a prior claim on your affections," she said coldly, though her heart was beginning to pound aggravatingly as he stood so close to her, his eyes fixed on her face. "I really would much prefer it if you were to marry her." She despised herself for the strange treacherous twinge of jealousy she felt again at the thought of Margaret and Duncan together.

He let out a shout of laughter at her words. "I've no doubt you would prefer it, my dear. Unfortunately for you his grace the king had other ideas, and so," he looked at her for a moment, "have I." He stuck the dirk into his belt.

For a moment she thought he was going to kiss her again. The blood began to pound in her temples, and she stepped back until she was leaning against the cold sill of the embrasure to the window. Then she heard the latch of the door lifting and she saw Marjorie peering into the room.

The girl gave a little frightened exclamation when she saw Duncan and made as if to leave again, but stepping away from Isabel he called out to her, casually dusting an imaginary fleck from the sleeve of his leather doublet.

"Come in, girl, come in. I want to see for myself the best needlewoman in the kingdom."

The puzzled astonishment on Marjorie's face was plain as she approached him across the room and dropped a curtsey.

"Needlewoman, sir? I'm no needlewoman."

"Oh come, why so modest?" He grinned at her amiably. "Your mistress here tells me that you're an expert with the embroidery needle. You must speak with my mother. She has every respect for people who share her skill in that. I shall arrange it."

If he heard Isabel's gasp of horror he ignored it. He merely turned to her with a small bow. "I think the summons to the hall for the noonday meal will sound very soon now. Perhaps you had better tidy yourself, my dear. I shall see you there."

Marjorie shut the door after him, open-mouthed. "What gave you the idea to tell him that? You know I can't sew. I must be the only woman in the kingdom who can't. Lord, my lady, now what's the matter?"

Isabel had sunk, giggling quietly, on to a stool. Speechlessly she shook her head. The shock of the happenings of that morning must have begun to make her light-headed, she thought weakly as she looked up at her affronted maid.

"He wanted to send you away, Marjie," she managed to say at last. "He wants to marry me next week, and I had to think of something to gain time for us, so I said that I needed wedding clothes. I said you were the best seamstress in the kingdom and he'd better let me keep you to make my clothes all the more quickly."

"Lor' a mercy!" commented Marjorie succinctly. "And he believed you?"

"No." Isabel began to giggle again. "No, I don't think he did."

In contrast to its earlier quietness, the Great Hall was packed with noisy people when Isabel and Marjorie made their way down to eat. Isabel found herself placed at the high table in the position of honour next to Duncan. On his other side sat his mother, and two places down on Isabel's right, on the far side of a large humorous clerk in black, sat Margaret Stewart. She gave no sign of having noticed Isabel; nor did Lady Crawfurd.

Isabel could feel all eyes in the hall at the lower tables fixed on her as she took her seat in the elaborately carved chair which was pulled out for her, and dipped her fingers in the bowl of rose-water presented by the page at her elbow.

Marjorie had found her way to a table somewhere just below the dais, and she too was looking up at her mistress, admiring the way Isabel sat so serenely in the place of honour, a beautiful, slender figure next to the powerful dark presence of the Master of Glencarnie.

Inside, though, Isabel felt anything but serene. She only picked at the food which was brought to her, every now and then sipping the Rhenish wine in her goblet. She was desperately conscious of the hatred of the two women who were sitting nearest to her, and felt almost grateful that her seat next to Duncan gave her protection against any further conversation with either of them. She glanced at his aquiline profile. She both hated and feared this man who was destined, unless she managed to escape him, to become her husband, so what was this power he seemed to exert over her; why did she feel this breathless excitement whenever he came near? Even at this moment, when he was leaning across to talk to the priest, his eyes fixed on the man's laughing moon face, she could feel it, a strange powerful current running through her veins. She had never felt this at any man's touch before – not even her poor dear Andrew, for whom her feelings were gentle and romantic and longing – and it terrified her. Surely this must be how a rabbit felt before the cold eyes of the rearing snake. She felt herself shiver slightly and at once Duncan's glance was on her again.

"Are you cold, my dear?" His eyes had resumed their hard, mocking expression.

She shook her head. "A shadow passing over my grave, that's all."

"Indeed. I must show you where your grave will be. We lie together, the Glencarnies and their wives, in the chapel here."

She shuddered convulsively at his words and he laughed out loud. Then Lady Crawfurd suddenly leaned forward round her son.

"My son feels that after the meal I should show you my garden, my lady." There was no smile or softening of the expression to make the invitation friendly. The old woman's face, framed in the stark whiteness of her wimple, had the same strong masculine bone structure as her son's, and it looked at the moment as uncompromising, but sure enough, when the meal was at last over she took Isabel's arm and led her slowly from the hall. Behind her Isabel saw out of the corner of her eye that Duncan had waited to take Margaret's hand in his. They were laughing together quietly.

Lady Crawfurd's garden was bounded on the north and west sides by a low wall which had been built out of the rock at the top of the high cliffs that guarded that side of the castle. It was bright with gilly-flowers and late roses and michaelmas daisies, and fragrant with beds of herbs cut into the emerald turf. Isabel couldn't restrain her exclamation of surprise and delight as she followed the old lady up the staircase in the grey wall that led to this rampart garden.

Lady Crawfurd turned and looked at her, her eyes narrowed. "You like flowers?"

Isabel nodded. "I have – had – my own garden at Strathblair."

The woman's eyes blazed at once at the mention of the hated name. "You surprise me. I should have thought that your father would have had very little time for such fripperies," she commented acidly. She made her way to a wooden bench overhung with full-blown pink roses, and sat down, arranging her dark velvet skirts around her.

Isabel stood uncertainly before her, not daring either to sit down or to walk away, wondering why the woman had brought her up here alone. The sun had grown quite strong by now and warmed her comfortingly through the fine material of her kirtle and gown. She could smell the turf and the herbs and flowers all round her, delicious after the night's rain, and it reassured her. She found Lady Crawfurd's eyes on her face and she smiled nervously.

"I am truly sorry, madam. I didn't wish to come here and upset your household," she said humbly. "I'm sure if the king had known that your son was already betrothed to someone else . . ." She hesitated uncertainly as the woman's face changed convulsively. The hawklike features crumpled and stretched alarmingly, and she realised suddenly that Lady Crawfurd was laughing.

"Betrothed! My son betrothed! To Margaret Stewart I suppose. Pshaw!" Isabel thought for one moment that Duncan's mother was going to spit on the ground like a common soldier. "That woman is no more than his whore. He has no intention of marrying her, I'm glad to say."

"But she said . . ."

"Said! Said! Don't believe what she said." Lady Crawfurd suddenly sat upright again, her face once more impassive, if a little guarded. "When did she talk to you?"

"This morning. She . . ." Isabel hesitated, wondering whether she should tell Lady Crawfurd what had happened. "She came to my chamber and tried to frighten me with her dirk. She threatened to cut my face . . ."

Again the strangely unnerving shout of laughter from the other woman. "Then she's more spirit than I gave her credit for. You'll have to be more careful, won't you, you poor child?" she said mockingly. "It seems there are people on all sides of you prepared to stop at nothing to prevent you from marrying my son." She stood up. "I'm sure you have already realised that I am one of them. Well, now that you've seen my garden I shall leave you." For a moment she waited, looking down at Isabel — she was the taller by a span — her face cold with disdain, then she turned and walked slowly back across the lawn, a tall stately figure, her veil lifting slightly in the wind. She disappeared down the flight of steps in the wall, leaving Isabel quite alone.

So that's what she wanted, Isabel thought miserably. To frighten me. She's a bully; like him. Holy Mother, help me, she prayed desperately, sinking onto the bench. What am I to do? They all hate me and want to be rid of me, and yet, because of the king, I can't go; I'm trapped here. She choked back a sob. If only Andrew had got the message and could come for her! If only he could take her away! Soon. Even if it meant defying the king. She ached with longing suddenly at the thought of him, with his gentle hands and the quiet grey eyes, and the soft affection of his kisses. He was so unlike the Black Fox in every way.

A shadow fell across the bright grass in front of her and she looked up with a start. Margaret Stewart was standing there, a faint mocking smile on her face. For a moment Isabel was too surprised to move, then to her amazement, before she could jump to her feet or call out, Margaret had sunk down to sit on the damp ground immediately in front of her.

"Keep still. I want to talk to you," she said in a low tone. "We're quite alone here and no one can overhear us. The old woman has gone. You said that you would leave Glencarnie if you could. Did you mean it?" Her expression was inscrutable.

Isabel thought quickly. Had the woman come to spy on her for Duncan, or was there a chance she might be persuaded to help her get away from the castle? She took a deep breath.

"I'd go, if it wasn't that the king himself had commanded our marriage," she said carefully.

Margaret gave a small hard laugh. "Commanded! Who is the king to command our happiness or misery just because of a whim? Jamie Stewart! He's no more right to that throne than a dozen others. Why," she gave a derisive sneer, "he's a distant kinsman of mine! Oh no, Isabel of Strathblair, I don't intend to let him order me and my marriage, and no more," she suddenly looked very hard at Isabel, "does Duncan. So be warned."

Isabel was nervously pleating the material of her dress between her fingers. Margaret's outburst against the king had shocked her, but it had also given her a sudden surge of hope.

She looked up, her expression carefully guarded. "The king persuaded my father to agree to this match because he held my brother Ian as a hostage. Ian's safe now; but I don't know what lever the king used to force Duncan to agree."

"Neither do I." The green eyes glittered dangerously for a moment. "Leave that to me to find out. The point is, your brother is safe; the king has no more hold over him or your father?"

"No, but . . ."

"Then he has no more hold over you. You can defy him. If you want to." Again the piercing stare.

"But what will happen when he learns that we have disobeyed him, if I get away?" Agitated, Isabel rose to her feet, thinking of her father's plea. The castle of Strathblair, Ian's freedom, the Earl's life.

Margaret didn't move. "What does it matter?" she said coldly. "It will be too late. Throw yourself on his mercy, if you like. Tell him it was all my idea. Tell him that I bewitched the Black Fox and snatched him from beneath your nose, and married him first!" She laughed up at the other girl, and then reaching up she grabbed Isabel's wrist, dragging her down on to the grass at her side. Her face was suddenly hard and uncompromising. "All I want is your agreement. If I can arrange for you to get away, will you go?"

Isabel's heart was thumping uncomfortably. She swallowed. Then she nodded emphatically.

The other girl's face broke into a smile of triumph and – was it scorn? "Good. Now it should be easy. Duncan doesn't expect you to try and run away from him, so there are only the usual castle guards to avoid in getting you out of here. You're not watched in any way." She glanced round the empty garden. "It should be simple. Humour Duncan. Pretend you like him pawing you." She gave Isabel an intense look from her narrowed green eyes.

"You do, don't you, in spite of your virtuous struggling?" She smiled disdainfully. "Then wait, and I shall tell you when and how you will go."

"And once I'm out of the castle? Where do I go then?" Isabel frowned, deliberately ignoring the last taunt.

"What does it matter? Go home. Go to England. Do what you like as long as you leave Glencarnie!" Margaret brushed aside her question impatiently. She stood up and shook out her skirt, exclaiming crossly at the dark damp stains on her train, then, glancing at Isabel once more, her eyes hard, she turned and without another word sped across the lawn and vanished down the stairs in the wall.

Isabel sat still for a while, trying to compose her shaking nerves, wondering desperately whether she could believe all that Margaret had said to her.

The sun was going round behind the great main tower of the castle now, throwing oblique shadows on the grass around her, and glancing up, shading her eyes, she stiffened suddenly. A figure was standing in the shelter of a fall of hanging roses at the corner of the wall. She stared in dismay. It was the man Murdoch.

She began to scramble to her feet, meaning to call him over, but already he had slipped from his hiding place, and with a sly smile in her direction he had followed Margaret out of the garden.

Surely he had been too far away from them to overhear anything that had been said. Both she and Margaret had spoken softly, and they had several times looked round, she could remember clearly, to make sure that they were alone. He hadn't been in the garden then. Or had he? Thoughtfully she made her way to the stair and began herself to descend the steep mossy steps. There was no sign of him anywhere now.

There was nothing she could do about it anyway; she must wait patiently and see what happened, and pray that somehow a way would be found for her and Marjorie to slip out of the castle and having done so to meet Andrew if he came. Or if he didn't – and she forced herself to face the possibility that he might not – to find their way to safety without him.

Isabel found Marjorie in their room in the Drum Tower.

"Marjie, I've so much to tell you. There's a chance . . ." She broke off abruptly and looked around. Marjorie was standing in the midst of a pile of boxes and chests. Several had been thrown open to reveal furs and damasks, kerseys and silks. A further pile of materials had been heaped on the bed, and a large basket of embroidery silks of bright colours lay on the table.

Isabel gasped. "Where did all this come from?"

"*He* sent them."

"But why?"

"For your bride-chest, of course. The man who brought them up here came and found me especially and said that Sir Duncan had sent me a message. I'm to start stitching straight away and he'll send a team of sewing maids for me to direct." Her eyes filled suddenly with tears. "You know I'm no good with a needle, my lady. What am I to do?"

Isabel stared round aghast. Then suddenly the humour of the situation began to dawn on her and in spite of herself she felt her lips begin to twitch with laughter. "I think, Marjie, that Sir Duncan has tried to play a little joke on us," she gurgled, fingering a bolt of cloth longingly. It was an exquisite scarlet of the most expensive dye. Beside it were bales of saffron and indigo and watchet green.

She lowered her voice. "But we shall have the last laugh, Marjie. We're going. Lady Margaret is going to help find a way out of the castle for us."

Marjorie snorted. "Aha, your presence threatens her plans. She doesn't dare try and kill you again after what happened this morning, so the next best thing is to get you away so she can throw herself into his arms unchallenged."

Isabel nodded, refusing to let herself picture Margaret in Duncan's arms.

She looked round the room again. "We'll have to pretend to make a start on the sewing, Marjie." Regretfully she picked up a length of damask and draped it against herself. "I'll direct the sewing girls when they come. They can make a start on a couple of gowns for me – they can always give them to the poor if I've gone, and you – I know what we'll do about you." On inspiration she went to one of her own coffers and picked out a shift. "Tear a bit from the hem of this, Marjie. That's right. Now let me bind it round your hand. There. We'll say you injured it so you can't possibly sew for a few days." She laughed quietly.

Marjorie glanced up at her mistress's face. The frightened, drawn look which had lurked there ever since their ride down from the north had disappeared now that there was a hope of escape, and the girl looked almost cheerful as she knotted the makeshift bandage around her maid's hand.

That evening when she took her place at Sir Duncan's side at the long table in the hall Isabel turned to him with a smile.

"I must thank you, Sir Duncan, for the lovely materials."

He looked at her quizzically "I trust that there will be enough there for your purposes"

"More than enough." She glanced down at her plate. "I can't help wondering where it all came from, sir, so quickly."

He chuckled. "I raided the castle store-rooms. There will be no hangings or clothes or bed linen or altar cloths in this castle for a twelvemonth, but my wife will be beautifully dressed."

She hid her smile in her napkin. "Marjorie was quite overcome, sir."

"So I see." He glanced significantly down at the lower table where Marjorie was sitting, her bandaged fingers resting on the board in front of her "I trust that her injury will not incommode her for too long."

Isabel blushed. His sharp eyes had missed nothing, it seemed. "They'll heal very quickly, Sir Duncan," she murmured.

"I hope so. Otherwise there will be no purpose in her continued stay and she can return north after all," he returned pointedly and he smiled down at her, his brown eyes glinting with triumph.

Below them a trio of musicians took the floor immediately in front of the dais. The hall was growing hot and smoky from the burning flares on the walls and the candles on the high table, and the gentle tenor melancholy of the tune played by the men began almost at once to lull the noisy conversation and clatter which had filled the air. Isabel sat back quietly, waving away the succession of dishes which were brought to her after she had nibbled at the first one or two, grateful that Duncan had turned at last to speak to his mother.

She was weary after the strain of her first full day at Glencarnie and longed for the moment when she could leave the high table and creep away alone to her chamber in the Drum Tower. Twice she felt her head begin to fall forward sleepily, and twice she raised it quickly, hoping that no one had noticed. She pushed away the dish of marchpane sweets in front of her and lay back in her chair, closing her eyes for a moment against the glare from the candelabra. Then suddenly she tensed. Duncan had turned back to her from his mother, and noticing that her eyes had closed had gently slid his arm around behind her shoulders, and before she could protest he had drawn her towards him until her head was resting on his breast.

She struggled to sit up, conscious at once of Margaret's burning stare, but his grip on her tightened, holding her against him so that she was forced to lie there tautly conscious of the arm which lay behind her shoulders and the strong beating of his heart as her head rested on the amber velvet of the doublet beneath his gown. She could see other heads turned towards her now from the smoky depths of the hall; she knew Lady Crawfurd must be watching as well as Margaret and she clenched her fists in the effort to stop herself leaping to her feet.

Then the tone of the music changed. The players swung into a gay *basse danse* and she could hear the forms and benches being pushed back as the men and women cleared a space in the centre of the floor for dancing. The music swept over her, singing in the dark rafters of the hall, carrying her with it, relaxing her, soothing her indignation.

Duncan did not attempt to talk to her as he sat there and now that she had stopped struggling against him his grip had eased and she had to admit to herself that it was comfortable, lying in the crook of his arm. The strange excitement of his touch was not altogether unpleasant. She listened sleepily as the dancing notes of the trumpet and shawms surrounded her and after a while she could feel her eyes once again beginning to close.

She was jolted to wakefulness by Margaret's voice, immediately behind her. "Sir Duncan, as your bride is obviously too tired to join the dancing, perhaps you would partner me – as usual."

Isabel pushed herself upright. She could see the amused glance of Lady Crawfurd across Duncan's shoulder. He did not move his arm from behind her, but he half turned to look up at Margaret. "Not tonight, I think, Margaret. It would scarcely be courteous to our guest." His voice was light and polite.

Margaret was finding it hard to keep a rein on her anger. "It is scarce polite to me either, sir. You discard the partner of months, and scorn me before the whole hall! People have noticed, Duncan, and already I have been mocked." She clenched her teeth. "You could do much to redeem my honour before your household if you would dance with me now."

Although Isabel was trying to struggle free of his arm, still he wouldn't move it. He grinned up at Margaret amiably, obviously enjoying the situation.

"So the lovely Margaret Stewart has to beg for a dancing partner to redeem her honour; Lord! What a come-down. And, of course, if I were to dance with you it would show, wouldn't it, my dear, that I still prefer your charms to those of my intended wife, which would be a triumph!"

Isabel was seriously alarmed. Although Margaret herself had suggested that very afternoon that she allow Duncan's attentions, she didn't want to antagonise the woman who might hold the only key to her escape. She made a supreme effort and at last managed to push back her chair and rise to her feet, throwing off his arm.

"Please, Sir Duncan, dance with lady Margaret. I am too tired. I would much rather go to bed."

Always in the background she could see the amused, arrogant face of Duncan's mother, strangely dark in the flickering candlelight, watching them.

Duncan rose beside her "Murdoch, my Lady Margaret wishes to dance. Will you partner her in the *basse danse*," he called down the table, in a voice which carried well into the hall. Margaret blushed angrily. Then he turned to Isabel. "I shall escort you to your chamber, my dear. Come." And he took her arm.

It was no good protesting. She caught sight of Margaret's furious glare as he led her towards the back of the dais to the door to the courtyard, his fingers gripping her wrist so that she could not pull free. She saw Murdoch approach the angry woman with an elegant bow and lead her down from the dais into the body of the hall, and then Duncan pulled open the door and they were outside. No one followed them.

It had begun to rain, soaking her gown in seconds as she stood behind him in the shelter of the eaves. He turned and swept her up into his arms

"We don't want you catching cold, my dear, do we?" he murmured as he strode out into the wet, carrying her easily with long firm strides towards the darkened doorway of the Drum Tower.

No one had yet lit the candle in the sconce on the stair. It was black as pitch, but he carried her up without hesitation, kicking open the door of her chamber. The only light there came from the dying embers of the fire.

Striding across the floor he laid her gently on the bed amidst the pile of costly materials which were still strewn there. Then he bent over her

She tried to push him away but he grabbed her wrists and holding them easily in one hand he began with practised fingers to unpin her head-dress. Her loosened hair glistened like a shining cascade of dark water on the fur coverlet, reflecting the small blue lights of the dying fire, and with his free hand he spread it out, weighing it in his fingers. Then he leaned forward to kiss her.

For a moment she lay quite still, overcome with the treacherous longing and excitement she had felt before when he touched her, but then, as she felt his hand beginning to work its way into the tight bodice of her gown, caressing her breast, she began to struggle at last, overcome with loathing and panic. With a convulsive wrench she pulled her hands free of his and threw herself to the far side of the bed, then blindly she brought her nails up, raking them desperately in the direction of his face.

He pulled back with an oath and then he struck her hard across the mouth. She fell back, stunned.

"Your first lesson, vixen." She heard his voice, lightly mocking, near her face. He gave a small spine-chilling laugh. "Teaching you the arts of love is going to be an enjoyable if dangerous experience, Isabel. I shall look forward to it."

He stood up and looked down at her for a moment as she lay trembling amongst the tumbled exotic folds of material and fur. Then with another quiet chuckle he turned and strode out of the room.

She lay still for a long time, sobbing into the pillow, her dark hair tangled loose about her shoulders, her torn and rain-soaked gown clinging to her shivering body, and at first she didn't hear the quiet tap on the door. Then as it was repeated louder she pushed herself up on her elbow and watched as the door opened a crack, revealing a line of pale light. A figure stood silhouetted in the darkness, candle held high, surveying the scene. It was Margaret.

"Did he rape you?" she asked, her voice cold.

Isabel shook her head. She pulled one of the fur coverlets round her as the pool of pale candlelight came nearer, lighting the bed, showing her disarray.

"It seems that my dear love is thinking to consummate this arranged marriage even before the ceremony takes place." Margaret's voice was acid. "We must get you out of the castle without delay." She set down the candle.

Isabel nodded. She couldn't bring herself to speak.

"Where's your maid?" Margaret demanded. "Dancing, I suppose. I'll have her sent to you." Her voice dropped suddenly to a threatening note. "Tell her never to leave you alone with him again, do you hear? Not that the occasion will arise. I'll see to it that you leave tomorrow. I'll have a message sent to you in the course of the day and you must act on it. There won't be another evening for you in the Fox's hall, I promise you that." Her eyes glittered coldly. "Tomorrow he will dance with me, all night, before the whole castle." She took up her candle again and with one last scornful look at the dishevelled girl on the bed, she turned and left Isabel alone in the dark.

It seemed like hours before Marjorie came to her. She was carrying a tallow candle in a holder and her red hair had slipped from beneath her veil. Her cheeks were glowing in the shadowy light.

"Oh madam, I've had such fun . . ."

She broke off abruptly, suddenly seeing Isabel sitting on the bed, her face streaked with tears.

"My lady, my dear! What's happened?" Banging down the candlestick she ran to her and took Isabel into her arms. "The brute! Did he come? Did he hurt you?"

Isabel nodded. "He carried me up here and tried to . . . tried to . . . Oh how I hate him!" Her voice broke and she began to sob.

"The bastard!" Marjorie spat the word out, rocking her gently against her shoulder. "The sooner we're out of this place the better." She lowered her voice. "What you were telling me earlier, about that Margaret helping us. Do you think she meant it?"

Isabel smiled wanly. "Oh yes, she meant it. She doesn't tolerate competition, you were right."

"Then we'll pray that she can think of a way, and soon." Marjorie smoothed the dark hair back from Isabel's face, then quietly and efficiently she began to tidy the room, stir the fire into life, light the candles and prepare her exhausted, frightened mistress for bed.

The next day dawned cold and blustery. It was as if the season could not decide whether it were still late summer with the balmy warmth of the midday sun on the grass, or autumn with its tearing winds and iced rain. The inhabitants of the castle shivered beneath their cloaks and wraps and cowered in doorways, reluctant to go out into the bleak courtyard in the streaming rain.

Sir Duncan had left early to hunt the wild boar with his men, so the servants told Marjorie as they brought up the fast-cooling water from the boiler in the kitchens, and she and Isabel breathed more easily at the thought. They busied themselves that morning by cutting out a gown of dark green kersey and Isabel herself began to stitch it as Marjorie, her bandage discarded, valiantly tacked the pieces together. Isabel was afraid to leave the room in case she missed Margaret's messenger, but the time for the midday meal grew near and still there had been no word.

At last Marjorie threw down her needle and stretched her cramped arms. "Shall I go down and see?"

Isabel nodded. "Here. Put on the bandage again. Go carefully. I must know what's happening."

She sat with the heavy green material on her knee, listening to the patter of Marjorie's shoes growing fainter on the uneven steps, and to the endless drip of the rain. Then she stiffened and frowned. Surely that was Marjorie coming straight up again?

Her eyes were fixed anxiously on the door as Marjorie reappeared. The girl put her fingers to her lips and quietly shut the door. Then she came and knelt at Isabel's side.

"They've put guards downstairs," she whispered. "They didn't see me. They were sheltering from the rain."

"Guards?" Isabel was startled. "Why should they?"

Marjorie shrugged. "Could they have guessed? Or overheard? Do you want me to go down and see what happens?"

Isabel thought for a moment. Then she nodded quickly. "Yes, try going out and see if they stop you."

She stood up after Marjorie had gone, letting her sewing slide to the floor, and went to gaze out of the northern window of the tower room. The others she had kept shuttered against the driving rain. Heavy grey clouds were racing out across the dark hill, and far below the wide Carnie was flowing in spate, its waters curdled with foam.

She paced the floor impatiently a few times, and once or twice ran to the door to listen, but there was no sign of Marjorie returning.

When the trumpet call to the midday meal sounded the maid had still not come back and Isabel began for the first time to feel afraid. Hastily straightening her veil, she threw her cloak round her shoulders and walked as sedately as she could down the spiral stair to the entrance to the tower. One man stood there, his pole-axe leaning against the wall. He snatched it up when he saw Isabel and she clutched her cloak more closely round her, but all he did was salute smartly. He made no attempt to stop her, nor, she saw as she hurried across the slippery wet cobbles, did he attempt to follow her. He merely watched as she made her way to the entrance to the great hall.

The hall was far less crowded than usual. Sir Duncan had, it seemed, taken a high proportion of his men with him on the hunt, in spite of the heavy rain. Lady Crawfurd too was missing, although Margaret was in her usual place on the far side of the burly cleric who, Isabel had discovered, was called Father Cuthbert.

She ate little and drank less, scanning the lower tables for a sign of Marjorie. She knew the girl would never miss a meal voluntarily, and there was still no sign of her as the final round of courses came in. Then suddenly she was conscious of a movement beside her. She turned to see Margaret slipping into Duncan's vacant chair.

"I've got a plan," Margaret murmured quietly. "There's a load of supplies due in from the village either today or tomorrow and it's possible we can get you out on one of the wagons." She glanced round surreptitiously, but there was no one close enough to overhear them. "It may not come today now because of the rain, so if you're still here tonight be sure to bolt your door. Duncan gets drunk when he returns from hunting and I doubt if even your chastity," she curled her lip disdainfully, "would deter him when the lust was up."

Isabel felt herself blushing at the girl's crudity, but she tried to ignore the remark. She looked down at her plate, wondering whether to confide in Margaret about Marjorie's disappearance. It did not take her long to make up her mind. There was after all no one else to whom she could turn.

"My maid Marjorie has disappeared," she whispered anxiously, her eyes fixed on Margaret's face.

Margaret was all attention at once. "How long ago? Is she trustworthy?"

"Of course she's trustworthy. She's been gone since mid-morning. She only went downstairs to see if the guards at the tower door would stop her and she never came back."

Margaret frowned. "Guards? Why should Duncan post guards? Has he any reason to think you'd try and run away?"

"I don't think so." Isabel blushed again, thinking of the previous night. "He imagines that I'm . . . resigned." She saw the slight twitch on Margaret's lips and tried to remain calm though her indignation was rising. "I did wonder, though, whether that man Murdoch could have overheard us yesterday in the garden. I saw him there after you'd gone."

"Murdoch!" Margaret sneered. Then she frowned. "He spies for Lady Crawfurd, I'm sure of it, although he's supposed to be Duncan's man. I wouldn't trust him for a moment with any secret of mine. But surely he couldn't have overheard – we were so careful . . ."

"Where is Lady Crawfurd?" Isabel interrupted suddenly. "Has she gone hunting too?"

Margaret raised an eyebrow. "I think, surprising though it may seem, that her hunting days are over. You're right. Where is she, I wonder? It's not like her to be absent from the hall, and she's never ill."

She turned and snapped her fingers at one of the pages

who had returned to the dais, after snatching his own
hasty meal at a side table, to stand ready with a wine jug.
He came forward and refilled her goblet. She whispered
something to him as he poured and Isabel saw him nod.
Seconds later he had set down the jug and was scurrying
out of the hall.

She tried to hide her anxiety as they waited, breaking up
a small sugar confection on her platter with nervous fingers and sipping every now and then from her wine.

Father Cuthbert was nodding at her side. She glanced at
him. In a moment he would wake and rise to pronounce
the grace and she would have to return to her room in the
Drum Tower. She glanced at Margaret who returned her
look with a cool stare. Neither girl said a word.

Then the boy returned. He seemed out of breath, but he
jumped nimbly to the dais and grabbing his jug elbowed
his way between Margaret and Isabel, refilling both their
goblets.

"She's in her rooms, my lady," he whispered to Margaret. "She's had food taken up to her there. She's been
questioning your maid half the morning," he nodded in
Isabel's direction. "Now she's got the girl locked in a
store-room. I could hear her crying from the main stair to
my lord's chamber."

Margaret and Isabel exchanged glances.

"Old witch!" Margaret muttered rudely under her
breath, waving the boy away. "I wonder if she's made her
talk."

"Why should she want to? I don't understand," Isabel
asked anxiously. "Surely she should be pleased if I left.
She hates me and everything I stand for."

Margaret smiled grimly. "Oh, I understand how her
mind works. I ought to by now. She hates you for being a
Strathblair, but never for one moment would she allow you
to jilt her son. No doubt she's already thought of a way to
stop the marriage, because stop it she means to, she's
made no secret of that, but her methods would not allow of
a Straithblair having the temerity to cold-shoulder a Crawfurd of Glencarnie by running away and making him a
laughing stock."

"How then?" Isabel couldn't stop herself asking.

"Either she'll try and turn Duncan against you —" Margaret surveyed her steadily for a moment, "or she'll think of a way of getting rid of you which doesn't lower the Glencarnie honour. For example, if you were to fall from your window into the Carnie you couldn't marry him. You would be dead!" She gave a small smile.

"Dead!" Isabel's voice rose in a frightened cry.

"Shush!" Margaret glanced round furtively. "Now do you see how important it is to get you away? If you want to live, that is." She smiled disdainfully and took up her goblet. "I don't mind either way, but no doubt you do. Now, you go back to your room when that old fool has said the benediction, and wait. And hope that the villagers bring up their wagons today."

"But what about Marjorie? How can we get her away?" Isabel asked desperately.

"We can't," said Margaret firmly. "There's nothing you can do. Forget her. Go without her if you have to. Ssh. Here's the grace."

They listened, heads bowed, as the old priest gabbled the customary words. *Pro tali convivio benedicamus dominum: Deo gratias!*

Isabel glanced up under her eyelids, but Margaret's eyes were closed piously.

". . . *Ave Maria: oremus. Meritis et precibus.*"

Almost as he was finishing Margaret had turned from the table without giving Isabel a chance to say anything else and she hurried out of the hall holding her cloak up over her head as the cold rain sheeted down. Isabel saw her disappear into the long range of buildings at the far side of the courtyard.

She stood by her chair hesitating for a moment as the other people who had been seated at the high table slowly shuffled out into the rain, then she followed them reluctantly to the doorway. She glanced across at the Drum Tower. The stones of the walls were glistening in the slanting rain and she could see the motionless figure of the guard still there in the doorway.

Well, she had no intention of returning there yet, whatever Margaret might say. She was frantic with worry about Marjorie and she wanted to ignore Margaret's advice and go and look for the girl, but good sense urged that she should wait. There was probably nothing she could do on her own and she might make things worse by trying to find her. To her intense relief no one else in the hall had paid any attention to her and behind her the servants were clearing away the tables, ignoring her completely as she stood in the doorway – but even so, she could not remain there for ever.

Then her eye was caught by the long lean-to stable block in the courtyard and she suddenly remembered her gentle mare, Muireall, to whom she hadn't given a single thought since she had arrived at Glencarnie. A visit to the horse would provide her with an excuse not to return to her room at once and give her time to think.

Gathering her cloak around her she ran out and over the streaming cobbles to duck into the dark doorway in the far corner. The stable was warm and fragrant with the scent of hay, and the smell of horses at once surrounded her in the half light. She could hear the gentle rustling of hooves in the straw and the chink of halter weights as the animals stirred and shifted restlessly in their stalls. Much of the stable was empty, the straw raked into piles, presumably waiting for the return of the boar-hunt, but at the far end in the dim light she could see the round outline of at least one rump.

She picked her way down the stable, holding her long skirts clear of the floor and at last, at the very end of the line, she found Muireall. The horse had been well cared for and her manger was full, and she whickered gently in answer to Isabel's whisper, turning to look at her mistress with her great dark eyes alert. Isabel went into the stall and put her arms round the creature's neck, miserably remembering that if she escaped from Glencarnie she would undoubtedly have to leave the horse behind. She buried her face in the silky mane, her eyes closed, comforted by the warmth and strength of the animal's neck beneath her arms, and for a while she didn't move.

When she looked up it was to see a wizened brown face gazing at her across the mare's withers. She stepped back with a cry of alarm and the mare flung up her head in fright.

A man was standing in the stall opposite her, a leather apron over his rough doublet and hose. He put his finger to his lips warily. "Are you the leddy who owns this horse?" he whispered gruffly.

She nodded.

"You sure?" He seemed uneasy, and kept glancing over his shoulder.

"Of course I'm sure." She stroked the mare's neck again. "She's called Muireall after the sweet myrrh.'

At the mention of her name the mare's ears twitched backwards and the man, watching, nodded, satisfied.

"I've a message for ye then. I went down to the mains this morning to collect some drench for a sick horse – the wise woman down there mak's a rare good potion – and I met a man." Again the groom, for so she supposed him to be, glanced over his shoulder. "Described this horse tae me, he did, down to those flea-bitten marks on her hocks and her brand. Said I was tae seek out the leddy that owned her – though how I was tae do it he didna ken."

Isabel's heart had begun to thump painfully. Eagerly she waited, her eyes fixed on the groom's face as he picked up a straw and began sucking it, as if still uncertain whether he should tell her any more or not. Then suddenly he seemed to make up his mind. "Said something verra' strange, he did. Said as how the makar would wait by the Leddy Rock at noon each day." He put his head on one side and looked at her inquisitively. "Does that mak' fair sense tae you?"

Isabel's heart had given a leap. Andrew. It had to be Andrew. He was a makar – a poet. Her eyes shone as she looked at the man across the back of her horse. "Yes, oh yes, it makes sense. Thank you." She turned to run from the stall, almost singing with joy and relief, then she paused, frowning, and turned back to him. "I want to give you something for your trouble – a reward." She had nothing on her to give. Then she remembered the jewelled brooch pinned to her girdle. Quickly she pulled aside her sodden cloak and unfastened it.

He took it eagerly, and before she could stop him bit it as if it had been a coin. Then, satisfied that it was gold, he grinned at her in thanks.

"You won't tell anyone else about this, will you?" she asked anxiously as with a wink he slipped the brooch into his pouch. He shook his head knowingly, and then with another wink he turned and slid out of the stall. He was half-way out of the door before she remembered something. "Wait," she called softly. "Wait, where is the Lady Rock?" But already he had slipped through the adjoining door, out of earshot into the next range of stalls.

She stood quite still for a while trying to calm her excitement. So Andrew was here. He had obviously come as soon as he had received the message and was waiting somewhere out there in the Forest of Carnie, going each day to wait patiently for her to appear.

She blessed the fact that providence had brought her to the stable to see Muireall that afternoon, for she dreaded to think what might have happened had the groom gone off to search for her in the castle, or worse still started asking questions. And it was so lucky that Andrew had remembered when he met the man how much she loved the horse and how she had always visited it every day when she was at home, even on days when the weather had prevented her from riding. He had assumed that she would do the same even at Glencarnie.

For a moment she had completely forgotten Marjorie in her excitement and relief. She gripped the silky mane in front of her and rested her forehead for a moment again on the horse's warm neck. Then, dropping a kiss on the fine white hair, she turned once more and stepped lightly out of the stall into the central passageway which ran behind it.

At the far end in the shadowy light of the half-opened door her attention was suddenly caught by a movement and she stopped dead.

Surely there hadn't been anyone there when she had

come in? The line of stalls had been empty and the stable completely deserted. Her heart thudding with sudden dread, she began to tiptoe down the passage between the empty stalls.

CHAPTER
FIVE

HER eyes were fixed on the dark space between the wooden partitions of the last stall but one on the left of the passageway. It was there she was sure she had seen something move. Holding her breath she crept nearer and nearer, and then the stack of straw in the centre of the stall seemed to explode before her eyes. There was a frenzied mewing and a black-and-white cat streaked past her, its ears laid flat against its head, its eyes savage.

With a little scream she leaped back out of its way, pressing herself against the wooden partition of the stall behind her. When she realised what had happened she gave a tense little laugh as she forced herself to be calm. For one minute she had thought that there might be someone there listening. She stepped away from the partition, straightening her cloak, and stopped, frowning again. The half door at the end of the passage was gently swinging open in the rain. When she had first come out of Muireall's stall it had been closed.

She flew past the last two stalls and pushing the door back gazed out across the courtyard. A sudden squall was sending the rain in heavy curtains across the cobbles, splashing into the doorways, carrying with it the heavy bitter scent of rotting leaves. She screwed up her eyes trying to see if there was anyone out there who could have slipped from the stable while she was distracted by the cat. She was still staring uneasily around when a fresh gust of wind caught the door and swung it back against its hinges. As she jumped out of the way she felt a little reassured. The wind was strong enough to have opened it if she herself had not latched it properly when she entered the stables.

There was obviously no point in waiting for this shower

to pass. All she wanted was to return as quickly as possible
to her tower room to think about Andrew. She couldn't
bear to think that even today he had been standing down
there somewhere in the pouring rain, peering into the mist
of the woods or the moor, waiting in vain for her to come.

She pulled her hood well up over her head and ran for
the shelter of the nearest archway, half-way to the Drum
Tower, but before she had gone a few steps she was soaked
to the skin and her thin soft leather slippers were squelching on her feet. She reached the dark doorway with relief
and dived panting into the shelter of its arch, shaking out
her skirts in a vain attempt to rid them of some of the wet.

Then she realised that she was not alone. Someone was
sitting on the bottom step of the wide newel stair which led
up from the small entrance hall. It was the man Murdoch.

He rose when he saw that she had noticed him and
bowed formally. He too, she could not fail to notice, was
soaked to the skin and his dark hair was plastered to his
head. Even the bright colours of his jacket were darkened
with moisture. He looked a little uneasy, she thought, and
she wondered at once where he had been so recently in the
heavy rain.

An unpleasant suspicion flashed through her mind as
she looked at him. Could he have been in the stables,
spying on her again? Her gaze dropped to his soiled buskins, but they were too wet to carry any traces of straw.

She smiled warily at him, still slightly out of breath
from her sprint across the cobbles. "It seems we're both
trying to find shelter, sir?"

"Indeed, my lady." His face had formed itself unwillingly into an obsequious pleasantness. "You have been to
visit your horse, I see. I hope you found it well cared for.
The Black Fox prides himself on the excellence of his
stables . . ." He broke off abruptly at the sight of her face.

"How did you know that I've been to the stables?" she
flashed at him. When she arrived he had certainly not been
gazing out of the arch, but sitting disconsolately with his
hunched shoulders towards the rain.

He smiled with obvious satisfaction. "Your gown, Lady
Isabel. It has hay clinging to it."

With an exclamation she glanced down. He was right; her cloak had swung open to reveal several wisps of hay stuck to the soft stuff of her gown and train.

She had turned away from him furiously to gaze out at the rain once more when a strange sound came suddenly to her ears. She swung round.

Murdoch had obviously heard it too, and he looked very uncomfortable.

"That's a woman crying," she said. She listened again. The wails were full of anguish – then suddenly the sound was cut off short. The silence that followed was for a moment uncanny, broken as it was only by the steady downpour of the rain and the splash of water from a broken gargoyle in the courtyard.

Isabel froze. "Where is this?" she asked with a sudden sinking certainty that she knew; that had been Marjorie's voice that she had heard.

"It's the Lord's Tower," he replied guardedly.

"Is this where Lady Crawfurd has her rooms?" She gathered up her skirts purposefully.

"Yes, but you can't . . ."

"I can. I want to speak to her." Determined, she pushed past him and set her foot on the bottom step of the stairs. The terrible sound of the girl's wailing had given her courage.

She ran up the first long curving flight of broad steps with Murdoch pounding behind her.

At the first door she stopped, her hand on the heavy ringed handle.

"That's Sir Duncan's chamber," Murdoch was panting anxiously at her elbow. "Lady Crawfurd is at the top, but my lady, really you shouldn't. You don't know how angry she'll be . . ."

But already she was running up the next flight. She passed two small barred doors – obviously store-rooms – and hesitated at each. As no sound came from behind the closed doors, she ran on.

At the top the door was slightly ajar. She pushed it open and stood breathlessly on the threshold looking in.

Lady Crawfurd was sitting at an embroidery frame, lit

by a pair of flaring candelabra by the fire, and with her were three other women, all sewing. Isabel could see at a glance that Marjorie wasn't there.

Four pairs of eyes looked at her with open puzzlement as she stood dripping on to the floor with the agitated figure of Murdoch peering over her shoulder.

She swallowed, plucking up the last shreds of her fast-disappearing courage.

"I have come for my maid, Lady Crawfurd. I understand that you are holding her here against her will."

Lady Crawfurd's thin eyebrows shot up. "Your maid? Why should I want your maid? I have more than adequate attendants of my own, thank you." There was a quiet snigger from one of the women who sat on a stool near the fire.

Isabel stiffened. "I heard her crying not a moment ago. I know she's here." She thought she detected a slightly wary look on Lady Crawfurd's face but outwardly at least the woman seemed totally calm. She leaned forward to her embroidery and slowly and deliberately inserted a stitch. "Pray search, Isabel Douglass, if you feel you can't take the word of a lady." Again the heavy irony without which the woman seemed unable to speak. "Try the garde-robe, for instance." She waved her hand towards a small curtained door in the wall, and there was another suppressed snigger in which this time all the women joined.

Lady Crawfurd suddenly seemed to catch sight of Murdoch for the first time. "What are you doing here, sir? About your business, man, quickly."

Isabel heard his feet on the stairs behind her as he ran down, not stopping to argue. She stood uncertainly where she was.

"There's no point in searching, Lady Crawfurd, I know that," she said quietly. "I believe you. She's not here. Now." She glanced round the room which was sumptuously furnished and hung with rich tapestry, but even so there seemed no corner in which anyone might hide. "But I must tell you that as soon as Sir Duncan returns from the hunt I shall inform him of what has happened. He gave me special permission to keep Marjorie with me until our wedding."

With as much dignity as she could muster she turned and began to descend the stairs. There was only a slight satisfaction in knowing that Lady Crawfurd's face had suffused with fury at the mention of the wedding.

At the first store-room door she stopped and tapped softly. "Marjorie?" she called as loudly as she dared, but there was no reply. She did the same at the second door, not even expecting a response, and then disconsolately made her way back down to the courtyard.

The rain had abated and already shreds of blue were showing amongst the windswept clouds. At the far corner of the yard a noisy gathering of steaming horses and men and dogs showed that the hunt had returned early. Two bloody carcases lay on the cobbles near them. She hesitated. Should she go and seek out Duncan now and tell him about Marjorie, or wait awhile longer? Her eyes were seeking his tall figure amongst the milling crowd of hunters, but there was no sign of him as far as she could see.

Her courage failed her at the thought of going to look for him and she slipped out of the archway and ran unnoticed towards the Drum Tower. She could always seek him out later if she had to, and already she was half hoping that Marjorie would be there when she regained her room.

But the place was still empty. Slowly and thoughtfully she stripped off her wet clothes and shoes and wrapped herself in her fur-lined bed-gown while she towelled her hair dry. Her mind was in a whirl – torn between her worry for Marjorie and her excitement and hope now that Andrew was so near Glencarnie. If only Marjorie would return. She wondered suddenly whether she should go and find Margaret, to tell her about Andrew, but she was reluctant to confide in the woman any more than she need. She still did not fully trust her – even though now it was more imperative than ever that she leave the castle quickly.

She found a dry shift and slipped it on, then went to rummage in one of her coffers for some hose. As she did so she heard steps on the stairs outside. She spun round as the door opened.

It was Marjorie. The girl's normally pink face was a patchy red and white and her eyes were puffy and swollen. She shut the door behind her and shot the bolt. Then she collapsed on her knees in the heather and began to sob very quietly.

Isabel took a step towards her, frightened. "Marjie?" she whispered. "Marjie, what happened?"

Marjorie looked up. She put a shaking finger to her lips, then she rose unsteadily and beckoned Isabel over to the northern window, well away from the door. She pushed her mistress into the embrasure and began to speak, her mouth close to Isabel's ear.

"The woman is a fiend. A wicked, unspeakable fiend. I can't tell you." She glanced over her shoulder.

"What? What did she do?" Isabel didn't have to ask whom Marjorie meant.

"She had me beaten, see." Marjorie half turned enough for Isabel to see the torn material of the girl's gown. "And then she pulled off the bandage . . ." Marjorie began sobbing again. "She saw it was a trick and she guessed why we'd done it. Sir Duncan had told her about the material. He made her collect it all up for you, which made her livid of course. She said I should make my wound more realistic . . ." Tears were pouring down the girl's face. "She had two of her women hold me and she took the scissors from her silks basket and ripped them across my hand." Helplessly she held up her palm, which was wrapped in a blood-soaked cloth.

Isabel gasped with horror.

"I fainted," Marjorie went on. "When I came to she was standing over me as close as you are now and she said she'd do it to my other hand if I didn't do what she said and if I ever told anyone." She paused. "She knows Margaret is going to help you get away. I don't know how, but she knows it. I didn't tell her anything – I swear it. She called Margaret all sorts of names, and then she said you must never go. She gave me a small bottle. Here." She rummaged in the purse at her girdle, awkwardly trying to use her left hand. "She said I was to put it in your drink at bedtime tonight. If I didn't she would know and tell Sir

Duncan we were planning to escape, and she said he would probably kill you if he knew."

Isabel took the little bottle into her hand. She suddenly felt very sick.

"Is it poison?" Her voice was shaky.

"She said it was a love potion to make you a dutiful and obedient wife to her son."

"And you believed her?"

Marjorie stamped her foot. "Of course I didn't believe her. But I had to pretend, to get out of there." She suddenly snatched the bottle from Isabel's hand. "Whatever it is, I never meant it to pass your lips, I swear before the Holy Virgin and St. Margaret, my blessed patron!" Whirling she leaned out across the broad sill of the window and hurled the bottle out, watching as it fell hundreds of feet into the roaring river below. "There!" She sank to her knees, her face in her hands, her shoulders shaking with sobs.

Isabel was completely stunned. For a moment she didn't know what to do. Then gently she knelt down beside the girl and put her arm round her. "Listen, Marjie. I've had word from Andrew. Your message got through and he's here. Already. We must pray that Margaret can arrange our escape this afternoon. She thought she might be able to – today or tomorrow, she said."

Marjorie looked up through her tears. "But how can we escape? How? You're guarded now. And it's nearly evening already."

"Margaret was going to think of something," said Isabel desperately. "She was expecting carts from the village and she thought we might be able to hide in one of them."

Marjorie gasped. "There was a big waggon in the court-yard when I ran across from Lady Crawfurd's room."

The two girls looked at each other in excitement. "But she hasn't sent a message," Isabel groaned. "Perhaps it's not the right waggon."

"Or perhaps she changed her mind about helping you. She's as bad as the rest of them, in my opinion."

"No, Marjie, she isn't. She doesn't care for me, but she

doesn't want me dead. She wants me out of the way so that when Duncan realises that I've run off rather than marry him she'll have him all to herself."

"It's my opinion you'd have died at his hand after the marriage anyway, once he'd obeyed the king," Marjorie cried out bitterly. "Like mother, like son."

Isabel gazed at her. Since last night she had not allowed herself to think of Duncan. What he had done had sickened and terrified her and suddenly, unhappily she wondered if Marjorie was right. She quickly put the thought out of her mind. They had to be practical. "Listen, go to the door. Don't go down. I've had an idea. Just call to the guard and tell him that I need a maid to help me dress. You can't lace my gown with that hand, and Sir Duncan," she hesitated only a second as she spoke his name, "Sir Duncan promised me tiring women and servants."

"But what good . . ."

"Do as I say. Tell him Sir Duncan promised me one of Lady Margaret's maids and he's to send her to me. It may be that she can't get a message to me because of the guards and if I ask for someone she'll have an excuse, don't you see?"

Reluctantly Marjorie rose to her feet and ran to the door. With her kerchief still screwed up against her eyes she relayed the message down the stair with as imperious a voice as she could muster. Then she turned and gave Isabel a watery smile. "I hope Lady Margaret understands what you want."

"She will." Isabel made herself smile back at the girl. "There is no other reason why I should suddenly ask for one of her maids."

The woman who came at last did not give her any cause to feel optimistic. She was a short dour female with heavy black eyebrows which met across the bridge of her nose. She was deft, however, and good at her job, and having helped Isabel into her gown and dressed her hair she proceeded to gather up the wet clothes and throw them into a hamper.

Twice Isabel tried to think of a way of asking the woman

about Margaret and twice her heart failed her, and then quite suddenly it was the maid who opened the subject herself.

"You'll have to send word to the hall tonight that you've caught a bad cold in the rain and won't be coming down," she said as she pitched Marjorie's blood-stained kirtle into the hamper and threw down the lid. "At dusk the drawbridge goes up and non can leave the castle. The Lady Margaret says you've tae go within the hour."

Isabel gasped. "Within the hour? But how?"

"Ah well, you're lucky, see. There's a waggon come frae the village in the courtyard unloading flour from the mill. You'll have tae lie under the empty sacks. It's risky, but my lady can't think of another way quickly. If you don't want to try it now, there'll be another in three days or so."

"No, we must try now." Isabel swallowed and glanced at Marjorie, who had gone white.

The woman nodded. "It'll be difficult getting you to the waggon as they've put a guard below, but we think we can work it. My lady says it's up tae you to how you get off the cart once you're out of the castle, and as to where you go, she doesnae want to know."

"We'll manage somehow." Isabel nodded. "Will you see that the message is sent to Sir Duncan in the hall for me; it'll give us a start if we're not missed – and if he doesn't come up to see where I am." She paused doubtfully as the other woman nodded.

"I'll see he's told. From what I hear I dinna doubt he'll be expecting it." She gave a knowing leer. "Now, here's how it's to be done. I'll send for the washerwomen to take this hamper. When they come you'll borrow their cloaks and aprons and carry the thing out yourselves. The cart is parked right by the wash-house, as luck would have it, so you can walk across the courtyard to it quite easily. The rain has stopped at long last, the lord be thanked. Once you're there," she shrugged, "I daresay you'll find a way to hide yourselves on it. The men'll be fair drunk by now, I dinna doubt!"

She finished buckling the hamper straps and straight

ened up. "Right. I'll away and send the lassies to you.
You've something tae give them? To mak' it worth their
while?"

Isabel nodded numbly. She hadn't expected everything
to happen so quickly.

Nervously she and Marjorie sat on the bed side by side,
gazing at the big hamper which lay on the floor near the
door. Then quickly Isabel got up and went to her box
of jewels and picked out two necklaces and a couple of
rings.

The sound of feet on the stairs made her fumble and
drop one. Her hands were shaking. She picked up a
handful of coins for good measure and by force of habit
put the box back in her coffer just as there was a knock on
the door.

The two girls were giggling quietly outside as Marjorie
opened the door to them. They came in with furtive
glances over their shoulders and giggled again as they at
once began to take off their cloaks. Obviously they had
been well primed.

"Here." Isabel handed them each a necklace and a ring
and a small handful of the coins. "Now please, keep silent
about this until tomorrow. Then you may say I bribed
you, or whatever you like."

"Nay, we'll not be caught." The taller girl had a pert,
pretty face. She began to tie her big white apron round
Isabel's slim waist. "The guard'll change soon. Soon as he
does I'll go down – as your maid – and later, so will Morag.
In the dusk he'll not recognise us, nor care as like as
not."

The girls giggled again as they helped Isabel and Marjorie on with the warm homespun cloaks and pulled the
hoods up over their faces.

"There, no one would know. If he tries to pinch you as
you go by you'll just have tae let him!" She went off into a
peal of laughter.

Then cautiously they opened the door and peered out.
The stair was dark. Picking up the heavy hamper, Isabel
and Marjorie tiptoed out.

"Dinna be so careful with it!" whispered Morag after

them. "We aren't!" There was another hoarse giggle and the door closed behind them.

Isabel could feel the heavy basket already making her arms ache as she clasped the handle with both her hands and she thought suddenly of the horrible wound on Marjorie's palm and bit her lip in remorse. She had forgotten about it and the girl hadn't even winced as she picked up her end.

Together they began to drag it clumping down the steep stairway, and remembering what Morag had said Isabel called back, trying to copy the girl's rough carefree voice, "Dinna drop that on me, you lummock!" and Marjorie replied with a forced laugh at once, "I wonder what it is they've got in here. It's heavy enough to be a side of bacon."

The man at arms was standing outside the archway watching the activity in the courtyard. Isabel was sure that he would turn, and every moment she waited, heart thumping, for him to accost them as they lugged the basket past him, but he scarcely gave them a second glance.

Her heart was in her mouth as she led the way openly across the slippery cobbles. No one took the slightest notice of them, and she saw that their heavy cloaks were identical to those worn by other servants and attendants in the bustling damp courtyard.

The waggon was standing at the far side of the yard, backed up against a large open double door through which they could see men throwing the heavy sacks. One man, dressed in a sturdy leather apron and hose, was heaving the last of the sacks down to his colleague below. The two shaggy bay horses were standing dozing in the shafts, their heads hanging low, reins trailing.

"Stop for a rest," Isabel hissed at Marjorie when they were a few yards away from it. "What are we going to do?"

They dropped their heavy burden on the ground and stretched their arms ostentatiously. "I don't see how we can get up there without being seen by a dozen people."

"There's the wash-house." Marjorie nodded towards a

narrow door near the cart. "I can smell the lye and wet
linen."

There was a shout of triumph from the man on the cart
as the last heavy sack was unloaded and he vaulted down
beside it. He disappeared with his colleagues inside the
double door and they heard a shout of laughter from the
men as the doors swung shut behind them.

"Now's our chance," Isabel said quickly. "Take the
hamper to the wash-house door, drop it and make a run for
the cart while there's no one near it."

They stooped to pick up the hamper and began to
stagger the last yards across the cobbles. Then suddenly
Isabel stopped dead — so suddenly that Marjorie was
nearly knocked off her feet.

In front of them, barely a few steps away, Duncan
appeared from a hidden archway in the granary wall. He
was dusting flour from his doublet and he looked grimly
satisfied.

Isabel bit back the scream which had risen involuntarily
to her lips and shrank back into her hood. It seemed to her
that he was looking straight at her.

"Come on, what are ye stopping for?" Marjorie swore at
her in desperation, copying Morag's shrill excitable tones
as she sensed Isabel's panic. "We'll be for it if we dinna get
this load in soon."

Her heart thudding with fear, Isabel half turned away
from him, as if to get a better grip on the hamper, and they
hurried on past the two sleepy horses. Duncan didn't
appear to have noticed them. He walked on slowly away
from them, preoccupied with some thought of his own,
and they peered after him fearfully once the horses were
safely between them, dropping the hamper at the wash-
house door.

"He's going to the Lord's Tower. Quick, now's our
chance." Marjorie grabbed Isabel's hand as her mistress
looked dazedly after him and dragged her towards the
waggon.

It was difficult to climb up hampered by their skirts,
but somehow they managed to haul themsleves up over
the great wooden wheel and tumble into the floury body of

the vehicle. For one awful moment they thought it was completely empty, then Marjorie saw a pile of empty sacks in the far corner. They were sodden.

"They must have covered the load with them," she muttered, pulling at them with frantic haste. "Come on, it can't be helped. We'll get dry somehow later. Under you go."

Isabel flung herself down and Marjorie covered her before huddling down next to her, praying that no piece of their gowns was showing. The bitter smell of the wet sacking was overwhelming.

The two girls lay there, tense with fear, for what seemed an eternity. Then they heard at last the shouts of the men from the granary behind them. The heavy doors were being dragged shut and they heard the bar fall with a crash into its sockets. The men had obviously been freely indulging in the castle's ale. Their shouts and laughter were raucous as they hauled themselves up on to the high seat at the front of the cart. Isabel, her face buried in the smelly wet sack, could feel herself beginning to shake uncontrollably as she heard the man bawling at his horses and listened to the whistle of his whip.

The heavy vehicle shuddered into life and rattled painfully across the cobbles. Supposing they were searched? Supposing a man-at-arms stuck his lance into the pile of sacks just to make sure there was nothing there? Isabel bit the back of her fist to stop herself crying out loud as they jolted forward.

The laughter on the high drivers' seat didn't falter. She heard one of the men exchange cheerful insults with someone on the ground and then the rumble of the wheels took on a strange echo. They were passing beneath the high gatehouse arch. The sound grew hollow as the horses plodded patiently over the drawbridge, and then muffled again as the cart lurched on to the mud track which led south through the woods towards Glencarnie Mains and beyond it to the village. They had not been stopped once.

Isabel lay quite still, not daring to move. Tears of relief were pricking her eyelids and cautiously she wiped them away with the back of her hand. The first and most dangerous part of their escape was over.

There was a quiet slithering sound near her and she saw, opening her eyes wide in the darkness under the sacks, that Marjorie's face was close beside hers. Carefully the girl put her mouth to Isabel's ear.

"How do we get off?"

Isabel pulled a face. "We could jump," she whispered. "Or wait for the village?"

Marjorie shook her head slightly. "They might give us away in the village if they saw us. We'll have to jump."

Very cautiously she raised her head. The three men were almost hidden from view by the high board behind their seat, the thong of the whip trailing out behind from where the driver had stuck it beside him. There was another shout of laughter, and the rumble and creak of the wheels didn't disguise a loud belch.

"They're very drunk," Marjorie reported quietly. "They'll never notice us. Come on, away to the back." She began to wriggle purposefully backwards, taking the sacks with her.

Isabel followed, then froze as there was a general shout from the three men in front. Her heart beat painfully. But there was another burst of raucous laughter and then one after another they broke into ragged song.

Once at the back the girls carefully sat up, pushing back the sacks. The track was passing through thick woods and the interlacing branches overhead turned the path dark.

"They'll never see us. Come on." Marjorie was standing up, pulling Isabel to her feet. They lurched sideways as the wheels passed over an extra deep rut and then Marjorie flung herself over the high tailboard of the waggon. Not letting herself stop to think Isabel followed her, scrambling awkwardly over the rough wooden boards and allowing herself to drop to the track.

She missed her footing as she landed and fell to her knees in the mud, but already Marjorie was at her elbow, dragging her up, pulling her towards the dark thick undergrowth where they crouched hidden, straining their ears for any warning sounds from the men, but the lurching rumble of the wheels drew steadily away from them, accompanied by the cheerful sound of singing. Slowly the noise grew more and more distant until it had completely gone and they were alone in the silent forest.

At once Isabel caught Marjorie's arm. "Come on. We must get right away from the track. We might be followed."

Side by side the two girls began to fight their way through the thick tangle of brambles which surrounded them, straining their eyes in the darkness. Somewhere nearby a jay blundered up out of the trees, screaming, and they stopped, clutching at each other in fright.

"It's only a bird." Isabel's voice sounded high and unnatural as she tried to reassure her companion. "Come on."

They pushed their way on until they reached a clearing in the trees where they stopped.

"How do you know which way?" Marjorie asked suddenly through chattering teeth.

Isabel hesitated. All round them the great trees rose silently with patches of thick undergrowth tangling beneath the gnarled trunks. Nearby they could see a grassy ride thickly covered with wet dead leaves, and the acrid tang of rotting beech mast filled her nostrils. Glancing upwards Isabel could see the sky a clear watery grey high above the dark clouds. If it had been a fine evening it might still have been light.

"The Lady Rock," she murmured. "Andrew will be waiting at the Lady Rock."

"It might be anywhere." Marjorie rubbed her arm wearily across her face. "North, south, east or west; forest, river or moor. How are we going to find it?" Her voice had risen in spite of herself to a miserable wail.

"We're not; not in the dark." Isabel forced herself to be practical. "We must find somewhere to spend the night first, and then as soon as it's light we'll set about thinking of a way to look for it." How, she didn't know, but somehow the certainty of her words was a comfort even to herself. After all it could not be far from the castle or he would not have chosen it as a meeting place

They began to walk as quietly as they could down the ride, straining their ears all the time for the forest noises round them. They heard an owl giving its wavering hoot somewhere ahead and a while later there was the short agonised scream of some small animal dying beneath its claws, while far away behind them they heard the bark of a fox.

The wind was rising again. At first only the streaming dun-coloured clouds above the tree-tops showed its gaining strength, then slowly the high branches began to sway, showering the dank dead leaves through the dark of the clearing as, slowly, the forest began to whisper and rustle. Isabel shivered, praying it would not start to rain again.

"We've got to find shelter for the night," she repeated doggedly. "At least it's not frosty, but we must find somewhere warm and dry if we can."

"I'm cold now," Marjorie whimpered. She was holding her injured hand tucked into the warm angle between her hip and her elbow, but it throbbed painfully and she knew it was bleeding again.

They walked on until the sky above the clouds was black and pricked with stars and still they had found nowhere to stop that was safe. The forest loomed black and threatening round them and they found it almost impossible to grope their way through the velvet dark. In the end they crawled in total exhaustion into the centre of a tangled hazel brake and clinging together beneath the thickness of the two cloaks they fell into an uneasy sleep.

Isabel only slept fitfully. The first time she woke it was suddenly, staring eyes wide open in the dark, her heart thumping painfully. She held her breath, listening, but there seemed to be nothing there, and after a while she dozed again. The next time she woke it was to the heavy patter and rustle of raindrops round them. She was painfully stiff and shaking with cold and she wanted to get up and walk around to warm herself, but she could feel Marjorie nestling unmoving at her back and she was reluctant to wake the girl. Far away above the sound of the rain she heard the lonely howl of a wolf. She felt a little prickle of panic playing round her shoulderblades as she strained her ears to hear it again, but there was no more howling, only the moan of the wind and the rattle of the rain.

It was dawn next time she woke and the forest was full of birdsong. She sat up painfully and crawled out of the shelter of their sleeping place. The pale sky was clear of cloud above the russet tree-tops.

"Thank God it's day at last." Marjorie groaned, following her slowly and straightening up, stretching. She unfastened her wet cloak and taking it off shook it hard before wrapping herself in it again. "What now?"

Isabel was pushing back straying strands of hair into her hood with frozen fingers.

"We'll have to try and find a village. We need food and someone must direct us. We'll never find the Lady Rock otherwise."

"It's a risk." Marjorie frowned.

"I know it's a risk, but what else can we do?" Isabel was trying in vain to shrug herself more warmly into the centre of her clothes. Every stitch was wet and cold. "If we stay in the forest we could walk in circles for hours and never find it."

Together they began to walk down the narrow path; it was well beaten, but whether by animals or man they couldn't tell, for no tracks could be seen beneath the thick layer of sodden leaves. Gradually it grew lighter and the tops of the trees turned from dull red to fiery gold as the first rays of the sun touched them from behind the eastern hills.

They had been looking hopefully for the smoke of a village, but as they turned the corner round a clump of dank holly bushes they came unexpectedly upon two men who were sitting side by side on a fallen log. The men, as surprised as they were, leaped to their feet, reaching for their bows which were lying beside the them on the ground.

Isabel thought like lightning as she saw the fear and suspicion on the men's faces. She held up her hand. "Peace, friends," she called in a thin wavering voice. "Don't come near. We're from the lazar-house." She saw their faces pale beneath their tan and she drew her hood more closely round her, glad they had both been so muffled against the cold that their faces were hidden. "Please direct us," she went on pitifully, conscious that the misery in her voice was real. "We are trying to find the Lady Rock, to make an offering." She threw up a silent prayer that with a name like that it might have the reputation of some sort of shrine, or if it didn't that the men would know no better. "We've lost our way in the forest."

She glanced warningly at Marjorie, who was standing, eyes downcast, beside her

One of the men called out: "You're close, good woman That way; to the west. You'll be there by mid-morning." He flung out his arm to point the way, then hastily he and his companion began to gather up the bags at their feet Isabel guessed with an inward chuckle that they had been poaching and silently she wished them luck with their catch.

"Pray, kind sirs," Marjorie broke in suddenly in a painfully croaking voice. "Can you spare a crust of bread to two poor starving sinners? The prayers of the saints will go with you as reward."

The smaller of the two men hastily groped in his pouch He produced a packet wrapped in a cloth and threw it on the ground

"Peace be with you!" he muttered, and he and his companion turned and hurried into the forest without a backward glance.

Marjorie pounced on the packet with a throaty chuckle "I dare say the saints will bless him anyway, poor soul!" She sat down on the log and opened the napkin. In it was some cheese and two slices of fat pasty. They sat side by side in the damp clearing and shared the food, then, feeling much more cheerful, they set off in the direction the man had indicated

The track was quite clear. It ran straight as an arrow's path deep into the forest, slowly climbing through the trees. Gradually the undergrowth cleared and more and more often as they walked there were views of the sharp blue of the sky and in the distance the blurred browny purple of the heather-covered hills. They walked fast,

keeping a wary eye open for any signs of life, but apart
from the birds and the distant sight of one or two nervous
deer flitting through the trees the forest seemed deserted.

And then the trees began to thin and they saw the Lady
Rock in the distance before them. There was no mistaking
it. It reared up out of the moors, a giant megalith, carved
by the rain and wind into the unmistakable contours of a
naked woman.

Isabel stopped and caught her breath. Then she
remembered their story to the men and she gave a little
chuckle. "I doubt if that was ever a shrine to the Virgin,"
she murmured. "They must have thought we were mad as
well as diseased!"

Marjorie laughed out loud. "I'll make an offering all the
same. Look, the sun's not even high yet. We'll be there
and with time to spare."

The last mile or two of their walk took no time at all,
with their destination rearing ever larger before them.
When they reached it they sat down gratefully at the foot
of the rock amongst the heather and bracken, staring out
at the surrounding countryside. The hill fell away before
them, purple and crisp brown, to the broad river valley
which bounded the thick russet and green of the forest.

In the hazy distance Isabel could make out the high
cliffs, crowned by the uneven straggle of towers and walls
which made up Glencarnie, and she shuddered as she
watched it, wondering if their disappearance had yet been
noticed.

The sun was warm on their skin after the damp shadow
of the forest, and even so late in the year it still had the
strength slowly to drag the cold out of their bones and dry
their damp clinging clothes. Drugged with exhaustion and
the tension of the last few days, Isabel found her eyelids
growing heavy as she sat there, listening to the throaty
bubbling cry of a distant curlew, and slowly she dozed off.

She was awakened some time later by the sound of
hooves on stones, and her eyes flew open. A rider was
trotting up the track from the east, below them, a spare
horse on a rein at his elbow. She nudged Marjorie who had
been lying on her back, her mouth open, at her side, and

the two of them watched, heart in mouth, as the figure grew closer, until at last he became recognisable.

"Andrew! It is Andrew!" Isabel scrambled to her feet and began to run towards him, her arms outstretched.

She met him half way down the hillside, gasping for breath as a painful stitch seized her lungs.

"Andrew!" She reached up longingly as he sat for a moment looking down at her from his horse.

He smiled sadly. "So you managed to get away, sweetheart. You know what this means, to defy the king's command?" He lifted his leg across the pommel of his saddle and slid to the ground.

Isabel took a little step backwards, hurt by his manner. That was not the welcome she had expected. She stared at him unhappily for a minute. He was not so tall as she remembered, and he seemed frailer than before – or was that compared with Duncan? Angrily she shook off the treacherous thought. His eyes were the same – gentle and kind. She went to him shyly, and slowly he put his arms around her so that at last she felt again the brush of his lips on her hair.

"They were planning to kill me, Andrew. I had to get away."

"Surely not?" He held her at arms' length and looked down at her with grave eyes.

"They were so." Marjorie, who had been tactfully hanging back, came up to them at last, panting slightly. "They tried to force me to poison her."

"Poison?" He directed his gaze at her over Isabel's head, shocked. "The devils! In that case, I'm glad I've come."

"In that case?" Isabel pulled away from him suddenly. "You mean you weren't glad otherwise? You wouldn't have come just for the sake of our old love?"

"Of course I would, lassie." He smiled at her again, the old irresistible smile. "I would hardly have risked outlawry otherwise, would I?"

Both girls gasped. "Outlawry?" Isabel mouthed the word fearfully.

"Well, I'm defying the king by taking you away. Now,"

he suddenly became practical. "Mount up. The horse will carry the two of you easily. I won't be happy until I've got you well out of Crawfurd's reach. We'll go south. He won't expect us to take that route. We're going to make for England."

He lifted Isabel on to the saddle of the second horse, and then helped Marjorie on to the animal's rump behind her. Then he swung himself up on to his own mount.

Behind them the curlew sent out its long haunting whistle and, far away, echoing across the forest, came the sound of a horn.

Isabel shuddered. "The boar hunt."

Andrew turned back to look at her for an instant, his face grim. "I expect they're hunting fairer game today," he said soberly. "You didn't expect him to let you just walk out, did you?"

She bit her lip. "They won't find us, will they? We've got a long enough start?"

"I hope so," he replied. "Come on. Let's put as much distance between ourselves and the Black Fox's lair as we can."

He dug his spurs into his horse's sides and wheeled it round into a gallop. Isabel felt Marjorie's arms tighten round her middle. "Courage, Marjie," she whispered over her shoulder as their own horse broke into an easy canter. "We'll get away. I know we will."

And as if in answer, from behind them, the clear call of the horn rang out again, echoing defiantly around the hills. Already it seemed closer.

CHAPTER
SIX

ANDREW kept to the edge of the moors, galloping easily so as not to blow the horses too soon, skirting around the western edge of the great forest of Carnie. As the sun crossed the moors a heat haze blocked off the distant mountains; they seemed to be riding in an inverted shimmering haze of blue and purple. Isabel could feel the perspiration beginning to trickle down her back beneath the thick cloak, but dared not slow down to take it off. She kept her eyes on the back of Andrew's doublet and urged the horse to keep up with him, conscious always of Marjorie's clinging hold around her waist.

Andrew drew up at last on the summit of a small braeside and allowed his horse to rest. He turned in the saddle and shading his eyes with his hand gazed back the way they had come.

Isabel looked at him anxiously. "Can you see anything?"

He shook his head. "It's too hazy. I can still see Lady Rock. I thought there was something moving there, but I can't be sure. Come on. Let's get on. I'm turning south when we reach that outcrop of rock about half a mile on and we'll take to the forest for a bit." He ran his eye over Isabel's horse. "He is going well. I dare say the two of you don't weigh much more than a man." He glanced doubtfully at the sturdy Majorie and grinned.

Then his face grew serious again. "Listen, Isabel. If for any reason we should get separated, remember we are going south. I know there's a pass through the hills at a place called Lang Meikle Rig." He waved vaguely towards the dark haze on the horizon beyond the thick forest. "Make for it and wait for me there, see. If we have to ride hard for any reason or if I have to decoy them away from you we might well get parted. No . . ." he raised his hand as she opened her mouth to speak. "No time for talk now, lassie. Later."

Gathering his reins he was about to spur his horse forward when again they heard it, echoing across the hazy stillness of the moor; the triumphant note of the horn, and immediately after it, something even more sinister – the deep baying of a hound.

Isabel felt sick. She sent a beseeching look at Andrew who for one minute hesitated. Then he drove in his spurs. "Come on – gallop!" he cried. "We'll follow the burn further down. The dogs can't track the horses through water, they'll lose the scent."

"But, Andrew!" Isabel protested as she bucketed alongside him. "The hounds may have been tracking Marjie and me on foot, I understand that. But the scent of your horses cannot mean anything to them. How can they still be following us?"

"Your feet and the horses' hooves must have left prints round Lady Rock. I'd guess that when the hounds lost your scent, someone thought of urging them to follow the horses, just as a chance." He laughed mirthlessly. "Glencarnie may call himself a fox – he certainly knows how to order hounds!"

Rested by their short stop the horses galloped well, breasting the summit of the hillside and then turning left sharply into the forest. They rode on fast, following the cool green rides, putting as much distance as they could between themselves and their pursuers, and then Andrew wheeled abruptly down the hillside towards the dim valley bottom.

Slipping and stumbling they urged the horses downwards as fast as they dared towards the rocky burn which had carved itself a thundering course between moss-covered boulders. Andrew paused on the bank, looking doubtfully at the foaming brown water. Then he glanced up the way they had come and made up his mind. "It's the only way. If we can throw them off the track we might do it," he shouted above the sound of rushing water. "Would to God it had been a quieter stream. Go carefully, a horse could easily break a leg amongst these rocks and then we'd be finished. Let your reins loose."

Isabel watched him urge his horse, hock deep, into the icy water, then desperately she kicked her own reluctant animal after it.

For a hundred yards or more they made the horses stay in that roaring burn, then as the rocks became too steep to negotiate they turned them up the steep bank on the far side back into the forest, breaking into a gallop again as soon as they were safely once more on the leafy tracks.

The roaring of the water had drowned any sounds of pursuit, but when they were again amongst the silent trees they at once heard the baying of the hounds. They sounded much closer.

Andrew swore under his breath. They had lost valuable time in the burn and it hadn't worked; the dogs must be casting along both banks to find their trail and any moment they would be on the scent again. He glanced back. Isabel's face was white as she clung to the neck of the galloping horse; there was no doubt now that it was beginning to drop behind under the combined weight of two riders and he felt a wave of angry compassion seize him as desperately he beat his own tiring horse onward.

Behind them the note of the hounds' cry changed suddenly to one of excitement and again they heard the call of the horn. Their pursuers were once more on their track and gaining every moment.

Isabel could feel the horse beginning to labour beneath her. She too had heard the sounds and knew what the excited baying meant. She dashed the helpless tears from her eyes and called after Andrew.

"You go on; ride on without us. Get away while you can; it's me they want."

He turned in his saddle, his face set. "Don't waste your breath talking," he shouted back, not even bothering to acknowledge the insult of her remark, "Ride!"

But it was no use. Her horse had no more strength. Andrew, not knowing the byways of the forest, had relied on speed, choosing a straight deer track through the trees, but now they had lost their only advantage to the hounds, and at any moment the horsemen behind them would have them actually in sight. He loosened his sword in its sheath as he bent low over the horse's neck. "Come on," he called encouragingly. "All is not lost yet."

Their horses saw the grey streaking shadows beneath the trees before they did and turned at bay, shying and rearing as the great rangy wolfhounds circled in front of them. In a moment they were in the centre of a snapping snarling mêlée of vicious dogs and panic-stricken horses. Isabel, struggling frantically to control her half-crazed horse, heard Marjorie give a sharp scream behind her; she felt the girl's grip slipping and in a second Marjorie was on the ground, with one of the great hounds baring its teeth at her throat. Andrew wheeled his horse with an oath and rode at it, his sword raised, trying to force the terrified animal close enough to beat off the hound as Marjorie's shrieks tore through the air – and then suddenly it was all over. They heard the imperious note of the horn close at hand and obediently the dog slunk away. In a moment they were surrounded and the lonely forest track was crowded with riders.

Isabel, dazed, saw a man dismount and pull Marjorie to her feet. She was still screaming and he slapped her hard across the mouth to silence her before throwing her up on to his horse in front of his saddle and remounting behind her.

Then he was there, in front of her: the Black Fox, in full armour, save for his helmet which was carried behind him by his squire.

Isabel began to tremble, but his dark face was impassive as he held his prancing stallion with a steady hand in front of her exhausted horse.

"So, my lady. No doubt you have an explanation for this little exercise?" His armour was totally black; unlike his men he did not even carry his own emblem emblazoned. His sword was still sheathed in its scabbard at his belt.

Isabel tried to look defiant, although she was terribly afraid. Somehow she forced herself to speak.

"I had hoped, Sir Duncan, not to see you again."

He looked at her levelly. "I rather assumed that to be the case. It's a pity my hospitality is so unwelcome, lady." He stared down at her thoughtfully for a moment, stilling his restless horse with a firm hand on the rein.

Isabel lifted her head and made herself face him. "Full armour, my lord? And so many men to chase such a pitiful quarry? Did you think I had an army waiting to fight for me in your hills?"

He coloured slightly, stung by her scorn. "For all that I knew, madam, your father could indeed have brought an army to escort you back to the north, though I see I was wrong to suspect that. Your father has too much integrity to so dishonour his agreement. This . . . man . . . would not have come with the blessing of Strathblair. You! Bring him here!"

He snapped the order over his shoulder and to Isabel's horror she saw Andrew being dragged forward by two of the armoured men and pushed to his knees on the path in front of Duncan's horse.

"So," his voice was iron-hard. "This, I take it, is the gallant swain who is worth a hundred of me."

Andrew raised his face – it was bruised and bloody and his arms were being twisted behind him by his captors. Without armour he looked a slight defenceless figure beside the men around him. Beneath the blood his face was ashen, but his mouth was firm.

"I am prepared to die for Isabel, Crawfurd, if I must, but if the king knew the truth of this matter, I think you would be the one to pay the penalty."

"Brave words." Duncan's eyes narrowed. "If you are prepared to die for the lady, I think we must not deprive you of that privilege. You!" He swung round to one of his men. "Throw a rope over that branch. We'll hang him now."

"No!" Isabel's cry of anguish stopped the man in his tracks for only a second and then, with a glance at Duncan for confirmation, he strode over to pull a coil of rope from his saddle. "No. No, please." She was sobbing now. "You can't hang him. You mustn't. It's my fault he came. Mine.

I begged him to come. He didn't even want to help me."
Was that true? She didn't pause to think, but Duncan
hadn't even looked at her. He was watching as the length
of rope was expertly thrown across a high branch. The
men holding Andrew were tying his hands behind him.

"No! No!" Isabel in despair threw herself from her
horse. No one tried to stop her.

"Spare him. Please spare him." Tears flooded her eyes
as she ran to Duncan, pulling frantically at his rein. His
leg, on the great horse, was level with her head. She
clasped at it desperately, her fingers slipping on the cold
steel of the greave. "Please spare him. I'll marry you
tomorrow. I swear it, only spare his life."

In abject misery she flung herself on her knees beside
the massive iron-shod hooves of the stallion, feeling the
weight of her loose tangled hair falling forward over her
shoulders till it trailed in the mud.

Duncan looked down at her at last. For a split second
his face softened as he saw her shaking shoulders and the
pathetic angle of her neck rising out of the rough homespun of the washerwoman's cloak.

He snapped his fingers. "Very well. Enough. Bring him
back with us to Glencarnie. I'll decide what to do with him
later. Mount up. You, Murdoch, hand the lady up to me."

Isabel hadn't even seen Murdoch, who was standing
near her in the clearing, but now as she raised her lovely
tear-stained face he stepped up to her. He was smiling as
he helped her, not ungently, to her feet, and then lifted her
up in front of Sir Duncan's high saddle. At once the
steel-covered arm came round her, crushing her against
his breastplate, and already his great horse was moving as
he set it at a canter through the golden glory of the autumn
trees.

The sun had begun to set in a haze of purple as they
galloped back across the moor, and it was already growing
dark and very cold when they re-entered the forest south
of Lady Rock, but Isabel saw none of it. She lay weakly
back against the unyielding steel of her captor's breastplate and closed her eyes in despair.

The courtyard when they rode back into the castle was lit by a hundred flares. As the horses clattered across the cobbles the portcullis was lowered behind them and the grating screech of the winch chains on the drawbridge made it clear that the castle was once more safe against any who might want to enter out of the blackness of the night. Or leave. Isabel shuddered apprehensively as, when they drew to a halt, she found that Murdoch was already on his feet at her side ready to help her to the ground.

Duncan released her at last and as she slid from the horse he was beginning to issue commands.

"Put the man in the pit for the night and lock the maid in the Drum Tower. Let someone see to that injury. Murdoch, bring the Lady of Strathblair up to my chamber. Now."

Already he was off the horse and striding ahead of them across the courtyard, his sword swinging heavily against his plated hip.

Murdoch took her arm and guided her firmly after him through the arch and up the broad circular staircase to the Lord's chamber, where a fire was burning brightly. Two esquires were waiting there ready to divest Duncan of his armour. Murdoch guided her gently past them towards the fire where a heavily carved armchair stood by the hearth and she sank into it, automatically holding out her hands to the comfort of the flames, too dazed to take notice of anything going on round her.

She was roused by a low laugh behind her. "Here. Wine will warm you more quickly."

She turned from her reverie to find Duncan, his armour already removed, wearing only his white shirt and hose and thigh-length buskins, offering her a goblet of hot spicy wine. She took it with a shaking hand and sipped it slowly, feeling the warmth flowing round her body.

She lay back in the chair and looked up at him wearily. "It seems that you win, my lord."

His eyes were suddenly full of gold glints in the firelight. "So I should hope. You didn't expect to escape me, did you, vixen?"

She gave a faint smile. "Why not? It was a good plan.

Or at least I thought it was. How did you find us so easily?"

He gave a grim smile. "Recognise this?" He held out something to her and she saw the glint of gold.

She took it, puzzled, and then gave a gasp of recognition. It was her brooch – the one she had given the groom in the stables.

"He betrayed me?"

"No. Your conversation with him was overheard. It took little persuasion to make him tell all he knew."

So Murdoch had heard, and he spied for both of them, mother and son, as the occasion moved him. He was indeed a dangerous man. She felt herself go pale. "What did you do to the poor man?" She glanced up, but Duncan's face was inscrutable.

"The Black Fox does not tolerate treachery amongst his household."

She shivered at the unemotional words, but dared not ask any more as he strode to the table to replenish his own goblet of wine. His attendants, she noticed suddenly, had all disappeared, and they were alone.

She sat up, trying to shrug off the numb exhaustion which clouded her brain, nerving herself to speak again as he came back to the fire.

"What are you going to do with Andrew?"

He took a sip from his goblet and set it down with a thump on the table. Then he turned to her. "You love this man very much?" There was a strange tightness in his voice and he did not look at her as he waited for her reply.

"Andrew and I have known each other since we were in swaddling bands," she replied cautiously. "I care for him as though he were a part of myself." She hesitated. Why had she not said she loved him? She frowned, conscious that Duncan's eagle eyes were now fixed on her face. And then she knew why. "I love him as a brother," she said quietly and as she gazed in misery into the rich depths of her goblet, knowing suddenly that this was true, she missed seeing the fleeting blaze of triumph that had flickered across his features and then vanished.

"I had hoped, Isabel," he said quietly, "that you and I

would be friends. I was prepared to trust you, but it seems that was a big mistake." He was standing gazing down at the roaring fire, his feet planted firmly in their long soft leather boots.

At the word something seemed to snap suddenly in her brain. She rose to her feet, her temper flaring. "Trust! Sir Duncan, as it turned out, it was I who could not trust you! You should not dare reproach me, or wonder that I tried to escape you!"

He swung round. "And what do you mean by that?"

"I found out that my murder was being arranged, that's what I mean. You would hardly expect me to stand around waiting for that to happen?"

For a moment he looked nonplussed, then his face hardened imperceptibly. "So you thought that, did you?" His voice was so quiet she could hardly hear it above the crackle of the flames behind him. "May I ask your evidence?"

She swallowed. "Oh, I had evidence, sir. Your mother had my maid beaten until she was terrified and nearly senseless, then she tried to force her to poison me. Luckily Marjorie is too loyal ever to betray me . . ." She broke off.

His face had blackened in anger and for a moment she thought he would step forward and hit her, but he contained himself with an effort. "Where is this poison now, may I ask?"

"We threw it from the window into the river."

He raised an eyebrow. "And then you fled?"

She nodded weakly. "Too many people hate me in this castle. Your mother; your servants, Lady Margaret – you." Her voice broke so that the last word came out as a whisper. If he heard it he made to attempt to deny it. For a moment longer he stood gazing down at her, then he strode to the door.

"You will stay here for the rest of the night. The doors will be guarded, so don't try to leave. I will speak to you in the morning."

The door crashed shut behind him and she was left alone. She didn't bother to get up and check if she was indeed a prisoner. She knew he would not give her a second chance to run away and if he had she did not have the strength to go.

She sank back into the chair and closed her eyes miserably as the fire slowly began to sink and the logs to settle into their thick bed of ash.

She was awakened abruptly some time later by the door opening. The candles had burned down and the room was almost dark. Duncan strode in, now wearing his brown velvet jerkin but with his sword still at his hip. He halted abruptly in the dim light, trying to adjust his eyes to the dying glow of the fire. Then he saw her, still sitting where he had left her in the chair beside the hearth.

"I have confronted my mother with your accusation," he began abruptly as she struggled upright in her chair. "She did not trouble to deny it. She is, as you say, full of hatred."

Isabel gave a little groan as she tried to shake off the sleep which still fogged her brain, but he went on mercilessly. "Your father killed her husband, remember. She has every reason to hate you."

"And my father killed your father," she whispered. "You have the right to be full of hatred too."

He looked at her, his face expressionless for a full moment, then ignoring her words he went on. "I have her promise that she will never try such a thing again. She knows that even the sacred bond of motherhood will not save her from me if anything should happen to you at her hand before the wedding."

"And after the wedding, Sir Duncan? What then? Once the king is appeased and the knot tied, will you not want to murder me yourself?" Isabel forced herself stiffly up from her chair, and stood facing him, her head held high.

His expression became hard. "No doubt you will tempt me to it, madam!" He seemed inexplicably angry suddenly. "Now, I suggest you use my bed for the rest of the night. I assure you its owner will be safely occupied elsewhere." He strode across the room in six paces and the walls seemed to shake with the fury of the crashing door.

She wrapped herself unhappily in the old brown cloak

and went to lie down on the high curtained bed. It was sumptuously appointed with soft feather mattresses and fur coverlets but she noticed none of them. Dazed with exhaustion and too tired to think she closed her eyes once more and was soon fitfully asleep.

When she woke the morning sun was flooding through the unshuttered windows, two maidservants were carrying ewers of steaming water to a large wrought metal bowl in the corner, and a tray of food was brought in behind them. She looked at the food hungrily. She hadn't eaten since she had shared the poacher's victuals with Marjorie in the Carnie Forest. Following the maids was another woman carrying over her arm a fresh shift and, carefully ironed, her finest gown of scarlet embroidered with gold thread.

She struggled upright, forgetting that she was still tightly wrapped in the coarse homespun cloth. "Where's Marjorie?"

The tiring woman dropped a quick curtsey. "Still in your chamber, my lady. She found these clothes for you, but Sir Duncan felt she should remain there for now. He has sent me to wait on you." She glanced away with a half embarrassed smile.

"Is she all right?"

"Oh yes, my lady." The woman seemed surprised at the question. "Oh, she's tired out – like you I daresay – but well enough. They've taken her food and ale and her hand has been properly dressed and bandaged. Sir Duncan ordered it."

"And Andrew?" She hardly dared ask, but the woman had a kind face which inspired confidence and it was possible that she might have heard something.

To Isabel's surprise she smiled at once. "Oh, I don't think you need worry about him, my lady. Really I don't, but I can't say any more so please don't ask me. Just eat your breakfast and then I'll help you dress."

Puzzled, but a little reassured by her obvious sincerity, Isabel found she could eat the breakfast which was put before her, and then she allowed the woman to remove her torn and mud-stained clothes. The feel of the warm water on her body was exquisite after the coarse sun-dried cloth which had been like board against her skin. They dried her with soft towels and then dressed her in the finely stitched smock and heavy, full-trained gown with its broad hanging sleeves and elaborate jewelled belt. Then they brushed out her tangled hair, anointing it with oil of rosemary. Over it the woman fixed a silken gauze veil with a carved silver wreath to hold it in place.

Isabel protested. "First do my braids, please," but the woman ignored her, gently settling the chaplet in place.

"Sir Duncan's specific orders, my lady," she said. "The silver coronet is worn by all the brides of Glencarnie . . ."

"Brides?" She swung round, nearly knocking the brush from the woman's hand. "What do you mean, brides?"

The woman looked frightened. "I don't know, my lady . . ."

"Perhaps I can explain." Duncan's voice came from the doorway. He took a step into the room and the three servants dropped deep curtseys before gathering their bowls and jugs and hurrying away.

When they had gone, he stood in front of her for a moment, surveying her closely. She noticed that there were deep shadows beneath his eyes.

"You wear the bride's wreath, my dear, because today you shall be a bride." He ignored her gasp of horror. "You made me a promise yesterday; that you would marry me if I spared your Andrew his worthless life. I have done so; so I have decided to hold you to your part of the bargain; Father Cuthbert is to perform the ceremony without delay. It seems that already too much has threatened to come between us. The sooner the knot is tied, the better!" He held up his hand as she was about to speak. "No! No more arguments. I don't care whether you have one dress or a hundred. Your mistress of embroidery," for the first time a slight twinkle softened the hard lines around his eyes, "has been incarcerated in the Drum Tower to perform her mighty task whilst you and I take our honeymoon. Now, I have to leave you for a while. Murdoch will escort you to the chapel at the appointed hour."

With a stiff bow he strode towards the door. Then as he

opened it, he turned. "By the way. Something to put your mind at rest on one count at least. It appears that your beloved Andrew escaped from the castle last night."

He did not wait to see what effect his words had on her as he swung out of the room.

She gazed after him for several minutes, unable fully to grasp everything he had said. One thing however repeated itself over and over in her mind. Andrew has escaped. Andrew has escaped. But surely it wasn't possible? No one could escape from a prison pit, never mind from the high cliff top of Glencarnie once the drawbridge was raised. She didn't understand.

She paced up and down the floor, chewing at the knuckle of her forefinger, but try as she might she could not see how it had been done unless someone had helped him. But who? Who would help him? She shook her head, puzzled, only thankful that at least he was safe. Then a thought struck her. He was safe. But what was going to become of her now? What possible escape was there for her? She shivered. There was no way she could avoid the marriage now.

Trembling, she crossed to the prie-dieu in the corner and knelt a little uncertainly on the cushion. An exquisitely coloured missal lay open on the reading desk, but her eyes refused to read the words before her, just as her lips could form no prayers. Everything was a blur before her eyes.

She had knelt there for a while, unable even to think clearly, when she heard the echo of several sets of footsteps climbing the stairs to the door. She rose uncertainly and turned to face whoever was coming. If this was the party to escort her to the chapel then she must at least confront them with a brave face.

The door was flung back and Duncan himself appeared, followed by three men. They all bowed gravely to her and she in turn dropped a low curtsey, wondering desperately what he was going to do next.

"Isabel, sweetheart, it appears you will have to wait a few more hours after all before you become the mistress of Glencarnie."

Why was it, she wondered sadly, that whenever he spoke to her his voice so easily took on this mocking tone?

"These lords and I have some important business to discuss which it seems cannot wait. I am afraid that after all you will have to return to your own chamber for a while."

He took her arm and steered her to the door. There was no one outside when he came out with her on to the stone landing. "You below there," he shouted down the echoing steps. "The Lady of Straithblair is coming down; see to it that she reaches the Drum Tower in safety."

She heard the muffled response from below and the clash of arms as some invisible figure jumped to attention whilst she gathered her skirts for the descent. For one fleeting second he looked down at her and smiled a smile which went straight to her heart and made it turn over with excitement and longing and then he was gone, pushing the door behind him, and she was left alone trembling in the angle of the stairs.

She stood there, stunned for a moment, indignant at her own foolishness. This was the man she had every reason to loathe and fear and yet one genuine smile from him and she was shaking like a girl in love. "And I'm not in love with him," she breathed angrily. "And he needn't think I ever will be!"

She glanced upwards, tempted to defy him by running upstairs to hide instead of going down, but then she remembered who had her rooms up there and she rapidly changed her mind. Resignedly she threw the long embroidered train over her arm and turned to make her way downstairs.

She was brought up short by a shout of anger from behind the door. Cautiously she stepped back. The door hadn't latched properly when Duncan had swung it shut and she could hear clearly what was being said in the room beyond.

"We dare not leave it any longer," a strange voice was growling testily. "You keep delaying, Glencarnie. It won't do. If we don't kill him within the next sennight we'll have lost the chance of doing it before he meets the ambassadors."

"We have to choose the right moment." That was Duncan. He sounded irritated. "You'll ruin the plan by rushing it."

"No. Stewart's right," a third voice broke in. "It's got to be soon. We're ready; the whole chain is set up. There's no good to be gained from waiting."

Isabel took a step nearer the door, her heart beating furiously. Who were they talking about? Who were they planning to kill? She held her breath, her ear close to the crack.

There was a sound of pouring. "Here, gentlemen." Duncan's voice again, unrecognisably silky. "Let's drink to our plan; the date can be settled later."

There was a chink of goblets. "To the plan." The toast was repeated and then someone added in ringing tones the words, "Death to the king!"

Isabel gasped and backed away from the door. Could she have heard aright? Duncan and his friends were planning to murder the king? She could not believe it. Why, only a few days before she had seen Duncan at the king's side at Linlithgow as one of his advisers and, so she had thought, his friend.

Then she remembered. He had not liked being there. She frowned. What was the phrase he had used? Dangling at royal Jamie's elbow. That was it. And now suddenly she began to understand a whole lot more. He intended to marry her at the king's command, perhaps only to lull the king into believing in his continued loyalty, and then when the need for obedience was gone he could be rid of her. She shivered convulsively, stifling a sob of disbelief. Though she had heard the words from his own lips she could not bear to think of the Black Fox as a traitor.

She sat down on the top step of the stairs, pushing a corner of her long sleeve into her mouth to stop herself crying out loud. She felt nauseated. She had always known the Black Fox was capable of anything, but she realised now suddenly, with a shiver, that the man who dared to plan the murder of a king would hardly baulk at the mere killing of a wife.

"My lady?" she heard steps on the stairs below her and rose to her feet quickly as the cautious voice called up again. It was the guard wondering where she had gone. She began to run down towards him.

"I'm sorry," she slowed to a more sedate pace as she met him and followed him carefully to the bottom. "The fastening on my shoe became loose and I feared falling if I didn't fix it."

Her hurt and misery at Duncan's betrayal were rapidly giving way to indignation and anger. So he had thought to use her as part of his plot, had he? Well, this delay had given her one last chance, perhaps, of not only escaping him but of thwarting his plans. Her brain was racing furiously. Somehow the king had to be warned, and soon. But how? She could do nothing alone.

As soon as they reached the warm sunlight of the courtyard she stopped and her escort paused with her. He had a fresh youthful face above the severe line of his armour and his clear blue eyes surveyed her with a disarming candour.

She smiled at him winningly and was relieved to see him grin amiably in return.

"Before we go to the Drum Tower," she said with assumed gaiety, "I must see the Lady Margaret. She promised me a lucky charm for my wedding. Will you show me where her rooms are? You can wait for me outside."

His grin, to her infinite relief, widened obligingly.

"Of course, my lady. This way."

Margaret lodged in the northeast corner of the castle. The boy led her without hesitation through an arch, up an outside stair and down a passage until he halted in front of a rounded oak door. He saluted her gravely and then knocked on it for her.

"I'll wait for you here, my lady."

She smiled as graciously as she could, her heart still beating uncomfortably. When the door opened she took a deep breath and stepped inside.

Margaret, wrapped in a velvet bed-gown, was lying on her bed, her bright hair loose on her shoulders. She looked up in surprise as her maid ushered Isabel into the room and slipped out, leaving them alone, closing the heavy door behind her.

"Well," she said. "It didn't take you long to get caught, did it?" Her voice was heavy with irony. "I hope you haven't come to ask me to try and get you away again." She pushed herself up on an elbow and looked hard at Isabel. "Your lover wasn't much use, was he? You never told me he was waiting for you. But I hear he fled in the small hours without even a thought of rescuing you. I hope I never have to trust my life to such a man." She reached to a side table and took a marchpane comfit from the small silver dish there.

Isabel was stung into fury. "He'll come back for me," she retorted before she could stop herself. "Of course he will. How could he come for me last night when I was in Duncan's bed!"

The remark hit home. She saw the sudden suspicious flush in Margaret's cheeks and the anger and jealousy in her eyes.

"Did you tell him that I helped you escape?" the woman hissed at her suddenly. "I'll deny it, of course, but if you did . . ."

"I didn't." Isabel looked at her scornfully. But already she was regretting her jibe. After all, she had come to Margaret for help.

"Listen to me," she begged, taking a step nearer the scented bed. "I have just overheard the most terrible thing. You must help me." She lowered her voice. "Duncan has three men in his room with him and I overheard them talking just now. They are planning to murder the king. Somehow, we've got to warn him."

Margaret sat up and swung her legs over the side of the bed, her face draining of colour. "When did you hear this?"

"Just now. Oh Margaret, what can we do? The king has got to be told quickly."

"Does anyone else know of this but you?"

Isabel shook her head. "I don't know who to trust. I came straight to you."

Margaret looked at her for what seemed like an interminable space of time and then she suddenly flung back her head and laughed; a loud raucous ugly laugh. "You poor stupid little bitch! Do you think that there is anyone in this castle who doesn't want the Stewart tyrant dead? The Stewart who is the grandson of King Robert and his whore whilst there still lives a single descendant of Robert's true queen, Euphemia Ross? Of course Duncan is planning to kill him; and many more are with him. And let me tell you something. One of those dreadful men," she mimicked Isabel's voice, "is my brother William. And he and I, my poor Isabel, are kin, very close kin, to Robert Stewart, the man who will sit on the throne of Scotland when James is dead. So now you know why it is that I would plunge my dirk into King James's heart myself if I had my way."

Isabel stared at her, stunned. "You want the king dead?"

"Yes, my dear. I want the king dead." Margaret turned and helped herself to another comfit. "And I rather think, now, that Duncan will find your death a very small price to pay for your silence, don't you? In spite of your pretty bridal wreath!"

CHAPTER
SEVEN

AFTER the first moment of stunned horror Isabel found that her brain was working again with ice-cold clarity. So Margaret was her enemy too, but there was one weapon she could still use against her and that was the other woman's open jealousy.

She forced herself to smile. "Duncan would never kill me," she said as calmly as she could. "You know that as well as I do. Don't pretend you haven't seen the way he looks at me." It was true; she had seen him looking at her, once or twice, with something – admiration? anticipation? and humour, before the cold mask of antipathy was once more clamped down. She refused to let herself think of that last smile on the landing outside his door.

Margaret's eyes narrowed, but she didn't say anything. She was watching Isabel closely.

"Shall I tell you what he'd do if you tell him I know?" Isabel went on. "He'll marry me all the sooner, because when I'm his wife he knows he can demand my silence, and ensure it if he has to. After all, it's not for ever, is it? It would just be until the king was dead." She almost choked on the words but her eyes never left Margaret's face. "He's not marrying me just because the king has ordered it, is he? If so, he would not have given me the Glencarnie bridal wreath. He could have just postponed the wedding – I've given him enough excuses." The spasm on Margaret's face showed the words had gone home. She forced herself to smile. "The truth of it is he wants me for myself."

It couldn't be true, of course; there had to be a reason for marrying her today. Perhaps to reassure the king or his supporters? Perhaps to use her in some way as a decoy? She refused to consider the question. Whatever his

reason, it was of very little importance now. The only
important thing was to get out of Glencarnie. Then somehow she must find Andrew and between them they must
warn the king.

Margaret walked over to the window and looked out.
Below, the tumbling torrent of the Carnie river roared
through the rocks towards the valley, the water an angry
spiteful black, reflecting the heavy burnished thunder-
clouds which were piling up beyong Carnie Law.

"If I helped you to get away again . . ." she began
uncertainly.

"Then Duncan would return to you. In his pride he
would not even search for me a second time." She mustn't
seem too eager. She must keep her voice light and casual.
"It was after all you whom he loved first."

"But you would warn the king."

Isabel took a deep breath. "No. I think perhaps you're
right about the king. I'm sure my father would agree with
you." She crossed her fingers against the lie, for she knew
whatever his angers and frustrations since King James's
return and his open rebellion at times, her father had
always been loyal to the crown. She shrugged casually.
"The king doesn't concern me. After all, he was prepared
to force me into a marriage I hated. I'll take my oath on the
rood if you wish that I'll not tell the king. I don't even
know where he is now."

Margaret seemed to be considering. Then, unbelievably, she nodded. She reached over to the bed table and
took up the little pouch lying there. In it the dirk winked
as wickedly as ever. Isabel shrank a little. So he had given
Margaret back her deadly weapon.

Margaret took it out and held it up before her by the
point, so that the jewelled handle formed a cross. "Swear
then. On the holy cross; swear you will not say a word of
this – not to anyone."

Isabel felt a prickle of superstitious fear as she laid her
hand on the icy gems. "I swear," she said quietly. Then
she looked up into the depths of Margaret's eyes.

"Did you come to me alone?" Margaret slowly returned
the dirk to its resting place.

"There's a guard waiting outside. He's supposed to be escorting me back to the Drum Tower."

For a moment Margaret considered, her head a little to one side. "He'll have to be disposed of," she murmured. She went to a door in the far wall and opened it.

There was a small turret room beyond the door and to Isabel's surprise she saw that there were two men in there, playing chess at a low table. They looked up as Margaret appeared. One of them, a thin-faced man elegantly dressed in ornate damask with a high dagged collar and full trailing sleeves, smiled. "Have you any advice for my bishop, sweeheart? He seems in a perilous position."

Margaret glared at him, pointing behind her with a sharp gesture, and the words froze on his lips. He stood up slowly and pushed back the stool on which he had been seated. Isabel could see that he was immensely tall and thin, his fair hair cropped shorter than was usual. He took two mincing steps forward, staring at her. "So, the Lady of Strathblair!" His lips formed themselves into a soundless whistle.

"The Lady of Strathblair must leave the castle, Colin, and soon." Margaret's voice was caressing. "Outside there is an over-zealous guard. I want him disposed of."

The other man had risen to his feet also. He seemed much younger than the first and was not so tall or so elegantly dressed, and his colouring was dark. They glanced at each other. Then Colin smiled. "At once, sweetheart. And then? What of the lady?"

Isabel didn't like the tone of his voice one bit, but she said nothing as Margaret went on:

"And then the lady, Colin my dear one, can leave." She glanced round at Isabel. "Dispose of the escort quickly and then come back here."

The two men brushed past Isabel and went out. She whirled on Margaret as the door closed behind them. "They won't hurt him, will they? I don't want anything to happen to him."

Margaret gave a short cruel laugh. "Why so fastidious, lady? Doesn't the Earl of Strathblair ever cut the throats of unwanted cattle?"

Isabel felt herself go pale but she dared not protest. They waited in silence for several minutes before Colin and the other man returned. There had been no sound from the stair.

"He's on the roof," he murmured with a smile, dusting his hands together lightly. "I'll pitch him into the Carnie as soon as it's dark."

"Good. Now, Malcolm Crawfurd." She turned to Colin's companion. "I want your hose and buskins."

"What!" The young man stepped back as if she had struck him.

She laughed. "You're the same height as Isabel. I want your clothes for her. It's as simple as that. Then she and Colin can ride out quite openly."

Isabel gasped. "I can't wear his clothes!"

"You'd rather I left you to your marriage bed, my dear?" Margaret's face was expressionless for a moment. Then suddenly she darted forward. She pulled the silver fillet from Isabel's veil and in one graceful movement had placed it on her own flaming hair.

There was a moment's tense silence, then Colin slowly began to clap. "It suits you to perfection, sweet cousin. I only hope Duncan likes it as much."

Isabel felt sick. "Do you think it will work – if I wear a man's clothes?"

"A man! She gives you more credit than I would, Malcolm," Margaret sneered. "Of course it will work. Now, change. Quickly. There, go behind the screen if you're so modest."

Behind the heavy wooden screen Isabel struggled uncomfortably with the lacings on her gown and slowly pulled the rustling garments to her knees. Margaret appeared, laughing quietly, a pile of clothes in her arms.

"Take off your shift. Now. First the shirt and then the hose." She watched as Isabel held out her hand distastefully for the still-warm garments and began to pull on the shirt and doublet.

Suddenly she straightened up. "My maid Marjorie. She must come with me."

Margaret put her hands on her hips. "Your maid! What about a confessor, and a cook? Who else would your ladyship like in your retinue? You stupid child, don't you realise the position you're in? Be thankful if you get away yourself. No –" She raised her hand as Isabel began to protest, "forget her. There's nothing you can do about her."

Margaret bent and gathered up the discarded pile of scarlet and gold. "I wonder," she said, "shall we make Malcolm wear this while you're gone?" And she gave another laugh.

"You'll have to cut off her hair," was Colin's first remark when Isabel self-consciously stepped out from behind the screen.

"No!" Her hands flew to her head.

Margaret raised an eyebrow but she didn't insist. She went to a coffer on her table. "Here. Take this net. Bundle it up and wear your hood well up over your face. Quickly now. And put on this huke." She reached out for the thick unbelted riding cloak which had been lying across a stool by the fire and slipped it over Isabel's head. It hid the shirt and doublet completely. She stood back and looked at her for a moment, then she nodded, satisfied. "Colin, send your page for two horses, and here, listen . . ." She stepped close to him for a moment and whispered in his ear. He nodded gravely, then he went to the door.

"Sim," he yelled down the stairway. "Sim! Bring my horse and Malcolm's. Quickly, lad. We want some exercise before the storm breaks."

He turned to look at Malcolm, who was sheepishly huddled in a blanket on the edge of the bed.

"Dare I leave him with you, cousin?" he asked with a snigger.

Isabel was watching, hot with embarrassment. The clothes fitted snugly, but they felt strange and uncomfortable, clinging to her legs.

It seemed only a matter of minutes before a scruffy page appeared. "Your horses are saddled, sir. Can I come with you?" The bright eyes looked pleading.

"Not this time, Sim." Colin stepped deftly in the way,

so the boy couldn't see into the room. "Come, Malcolm, my friend." He gave an exaggerated bow towards Isabel, and pushing the boy in front of him led the way at a run down the stairs.

Two horses were tethered to a ring near the tower door. Isabel followed Colin towards them, her hood pulled well up round her face. Malcolm's mount was a leggy chestnut, a full sixteen hands high.

She reached up to the high pommel as Colin vaulted on to his own horse and then she stopped in dismay. She had expected him to hand her up. Never had she learned to vault up as he had done.

She threw him a beseeching glance and, he seeing her predicament almost before he had reached his saddle, slid off the horse again, laughing heartily.

"Holy saints! I'd forgotten your wound. I suppose you want me to give you a leg up on to Favel," he called banteringly, loudly enough to be heard by the page who had subsided sulkily on the step of the doorway to watch them.

He threw her, none too gently, up into the saddle and handed her her reins.

"Follow me close," he muttered under his breath, "and keep your head down for the love of Mary."

The chestnut sensed the nervousness of a strange rider and it bucked, slipping on the cobbles so that she had to clutch at its mane, desperately trying to soothe it as they clattered towards the gatehouse and the dark archway which led out over the drawbridge towards freedom.

Sentries had been posted on both sides of the castle entrance. Colin trotted up to them and drew his horse to a skidding halt.

"Make way there, lads," he called, turning to make sure Isabel was still behind him. "We've an appointment to keep before dark."

To her amazement they stood to attention, stepping aside, and Isabel caught sight of a knowing leer as she peered out from her hood.

They trotted briskly over the drawbridge. Every second she expected to hear a shout from the castle behind, and she had to force herself to resist the temptation to turn back and look at the towering granite walls.

Once on the turf, heading for the forest, Colin urged his horse into a gallop and Isabel felt her own begin to stretch its long legs until it too was racing at full speed. She was breathless. She felt the wind pull her hood back and her hair tore free of the restraining net, streaming out behind her. Anxiously she tried to gather it in with one hand, but already they had turned out of sight of the castle, flying down one of the broad mossy rides of the forest, and for a moment she felt a surge of glorious exhilaration.

It was a long time before Colin began to rein in his horse. He had left the main track and taken a winding, climbing path which led up through thick tangling trees and undergrowth. The horses' hooves, muffled on the soft leaf mould, began to strike sparks on the rock which pushed up beneath the grass. Graceful ferns clung to the high bank on either side of the path, and the air was rich with the scent of damp rotting vegetation. They let the horses' reins slack, allowing the animals to pick their way up the steeper parts of the track. All the time they were climbing. Isabel glanced up. She could see the sky, heavy and ominous with metallic cloud behind the interlaced branches of ash and hazel. There was no sign of the sun and it was impossible to guess which direction they had taken.

She glanced at Colin, who still rode in front of her. He had not looked back since they had crossed the drawbridge, urging his horse onwards ahead of her all the time, and for the first time she felt apprehensive. Where was he leading her? After all, he was Margaret's man, even, she thought suddenly, one of her lovers. Had Margaret told him to lead her out in the forest and then murder her? There was a wickedly long dagger lodged in his belt. She thought for a moment of the honest, happy blue eyes of the boy who had escorted her from the Lord's Tower and she felt a rush of bitter vomit in her throat.

She glanced back. The path wound out of sight behind her, dim from the tangled branches overhead. There was no sound save the chink of their bridles and the thud and scrabble of their horses' hooves as unhesitatingly he rode ahead of her, threading the way through a maze of tracks and paths which always led upwards, winding through the trees.

"Colin!" she called out suddenly. "Colin, stop!"

He raised his hand, but he went on, making no attempt to rein in his horse. "Nearly there," she heard the words, muffled and distant, come back to her.

Her legs were aching; her arms throbbed from Favel's constant pulling, for he had a mouth like iron, and her moment of excitement back there on the forest ride had gone as swiftly as it had come and in its place she felt an exhausted dread as they rode on and on, thinking again with miserable guilt about Marjorie, left alone and at Duncan's mercy in the Drum Tower. Surely he would not avenge himself on a helpless servant. Silently she breathed a desperate little prayer for her maid's safety — and followed it with another, for her own.

Then, quite suddenly, the path they were on opened up onto a flat grassy clearing. The trees had thinned, and in front Isabel could see range upon range of dark desolate hills. Colin pulled up his horse.

"This is as far as I'm going with you, lady," he announced. His hand toyed delicately with the handle of his dagger and he raised one eyebrow insolently in her direction as he gave her a long appraising stare. "I trust your hair didn't fall down like that while we were actually crossing the drawbridge?"

She put her hands up guiltily, bundling the heavy locks back into the hood while her horse hung its head, blowing at the ground.

"Not until we were well into the forest," she retorted. "Where are we?" She didn't like the way his fingers played with the weapon at his belt.

Then to her relief he pointed vaguely at the mountain ranges in front of them. "That way is the south," he said. "I've no doubt you wanted to go towards the north, but as the king is presumably still at Linlithgow we didn't think that was a good idea. We don't want you troubling him, do we?" He gave her an acid smile. "Besides, I'm sure your adoring lover went this way, heading for England, so you'd better do the same. It's several days' ride, but the further you get the safer you are – from the Black Fox, that is." He grinned unpleasantly.

She looked at him aghast for a moment, her relief that he wasn't going to kill her disappearing in the fear of what lay ahead. "You mean I have to go up there, alone?" She stared at the mountains.

"That's right. And I don't advise you to try and follow me back. You'd be lost in the forest at once and I happen to know there are wolves around." He glanced up at the sky. "There'll be a storm tonight, I'll warrant, so you'd better find yourself some shelter before dark. Now, I'm going back, or I won't be home myself before the castle curfew; and I suppose that I'm going to ruin the remains of the material of my jacket all over again riding through that unspeakable undergrowth." He pouted down at the ripped sleeve on his damasked arm and gave a fastidious shrug. "Pleasant journey, my lady Isabel." He raised his hand in salute and then, turning his horse, plunged back in to the forest.

For a moment she had to wrestle with Favel, who wanted to follow his companion, so it was only when she had the snorting chestnut at last under control that she could turn and face the desolate hills.

She was near tears, but one small hope remained. What was it Andrew had said to her? "If we should get separated, remember we're going south . . . make for the pass and wait for me there." Surely that is what he would have done when he escaped from Glencarnie, hoping that somehow she would get out of the castle too and follow him. It was a slender chance, but it was all she had to cling to.

She looked round. Two distinct tracks led out of the clearing. Both were tangled with brambles. She gathered up the reins and set the horse's head towards the left-hand track. It braced its front legs and refused to move. With a sob of frustration she tried the other and again the horse stood stubbornly still, its ears flat against its head. She stood up in her stirrups, broke off a long ash withy from an overhanging tree and brought it down smartly on to the chestnut's rump. It leaped forward, snorting.

If Margaret and Colin had thought to lose her in the forest, and set her in the wrong direction for the king and for Andrew, they had perhaps unwittingly done her a favour. She was fairly sure that Colin, when he had said that Andrew would have come south, in fact believed quite the opposite, but she would show them. Somehow she would find Andrew yet and then between them they would – they must – find the king.

The path she chose turned out to be like the others, narrow and overgrown. She assumed that the tracks were all made by forest animals, deer or even sheep, but this one had been unused for some time.

The afternoon had become very close and stormy and she was hot and uncomfortable in the heavy fustian huke; her throat was rubbed raw by the coarse material of the hood. She glanced over her shoulder. There wasn't a sound from the depths of the forest behind her. She pulled off the stifling hood pushed it into the breast of her shirt and shook her hair loose on her shoulders. It was much cooler.

She let the horse pick its own way now as the path grew steeper. The trees were thinning and changing and she could smell the sweet resinous scent of juniper in the heavy air.

The heather flowers had died and the steep hillsides were black beneath the lowering sky as the path brought her out suddenly on to the bare moor. She stopped the tired horse and eased herself in the saddle, looking round. Ahead and to the left and right range upon range of lowering hills, dark and misty in the premature twilight of the coming storm, surrounded her.

She looked down at the ground, trying to distinguish a track in the thick heather as one or two late bees hummed gently amongst the few remaining purple bells. She licked her lips nervously. "Come on, Favel. Walk on, boy. The blessed St. Christopher must guide us." She tapped the horse gently with the withy and set it at a slow canter through the heather.

Lightning flickered across the horizon and she felt the glossy muscles on the horse's shoulder twitch nervously.

She pushed on desperately. They must reach the far side of the bare moor before the storm broke. She half wished she had waited in the trees but she knew that would have been impossible. Every stride of the rapidly tiring horse put another yard between her and the castle of Glencarnie.

The ground gradually began to fall away towards a wooded glen and thankfully she guided the horse to a well-marked track which led down towards a brown mountain burn. On the far side the hillside was lush with grass. She could see in the twilight the dotted white shapes of sheep grazing unperturbed. She strained her eyes to see if there was a shepherd who might direct her, but the hillside was deserted.

She rode down to the burn and slipped out of the high saddle with a groan of relief, sinking to her knees on the muddy bank, the rein looped over her arm, bending to bathe her face in the ice-cold water as the horse began to suck noisily beside her. Somewhere beyond the hills there was a distant rumble of thunder. She glanced round nervously. A group of rowans, still heavy with rotting scarlet fruit, overhung the burn and beyong them a hazel thicket tangled across the head of the glen. There wasn't much shelter, but anything was better than the exposed moorland.

The horse had finished drinking as she wiped her face on the sleeve of her shirt. The light was falling fast now and further down the glen, where the burn tumbled in a whirl of white water into a crevice in the rock, it was quite dark. Lightning flashed across the sky and there was a crash of thunder. The first heavy drops of rain began to patter down.

She led the horse firmly into the thicket and tied its reins tightly round the bole of a tree, terrified that it might bolt. She managed to loosen its girth with a struggle and it began to graze. She was hungry herself, for she hadn't eaten since early morning and she was weak with exhaustion and lack of food, but there was nothing for it but to sit down near the horse, pulling the hood up over her head again to ward off the worst of the wet, and rest her back against a tree, hugging her knees. She was very near to tears.

Slowly she had been realising just how impossible a task she had set herself. What real chance was there that Andrew would be there, waiting for her, even if she did find the right place? The mountains stretched mile upon mile and try as she might she could not remember the name of the pass which he had told her about. There must be a dozen places where tracks climbed up over the heather ridges and wound between the hills towards England, and it could be any of them.

And then with a stab of horror another thought struck her. How did she knew that Andrew really had escaped? She only had Duncan's word for it. Supposing he had had Andrew murdered and then lied to her to make her keep to her bargain of marriage?

Miserably she pushed her hair out of her eyes and gazed in despair up at the flickering sky. Some stubborn corner of her mind kept on refusing to believe it of Duncan, just as it refused to believe him capable of treason. The image of his face, the stern features relaxed for a moment into something approaching a smile, rose before her and she pictured him, his brown eyes flecked with gold in the firelight, his fingers resting lightly on her shoulder . . .

Angrily she banished the thought from her mind. She had the evidence of her own ears that he was plotting treason, and the king had to be warned at whatever cost. Whatever people said about him, he was the crowned and anointed sovereign, King of the Scots, popular with many, and her own father, who had every reason in the past to hate him, was his obedient and loyal servant and she should be the same. Somehow she must find a way of absolving herself from the oath of silence she had taken, and warn him, by herself if necessary.

She shook her head unhappily and closed her eyes.

The rain when it came fell out of the sky in sheets, bouncing off the water, soaking the undergrowth in seconds, penetrating Isabel's huke and hood with icy needles. It was pitch dark, but every few seconds the dazzling green flashes of lightning lit the countryside. Between the crashes of thunder she could hear the anxious bleating of the distant sheep over the angry rush of water.

Favel stirred restlessly, throwing up his head at every new roll of thunder, but he made no attempt to run. Perhaps like her he suspected that there was no other shelter for miles.

Then as abruptly as it had started the rain stopped. The lightning still flickered on the horizon, but the thunder died.

Isabel rose stiffly, untied the reluctant horse and tightening the girths as best she could climbed to the saddle from a fallen tree. She was too cold and wet to stay a moment longer in the glen. Her tears of loneliness and despair spilled over as she rode, pushing the horse up away from the burn out onto the hillside into the darkness.

She didn't know which way she was riding. For all she knew she was heading back the way she had come. Her hands and feet were numb with cold and she was shaking uncontrollably, so when the horse stumbled, his foot in a hole, she was quite unable to keep her balance and she felt herself slipping helplessly over his shoulder. She landed heavily in the soft mud and lay still for a moment, winded. Then, panic-stricken, she looked round for the horse. Without him she was lost, but he hadn't gone far. He stood dejectedly near her, his reins trailing in the mud.

She dragged herself to her feet, and cautiously approached him. He was resting one leg awkwardly, reluctant to put any weight on it. She bent and ran her numb fingers down the slender fetlock. It was swollen and hot. The horse was quite lame.

She led it slowly on. A high cold moon appeared above the heavy cloud and by its intermittent light she could see that now they were following a well-trodden path. The endless hills still rose in a barrier all round, but she could see signs of a break between them. Perhaps there was a pass somewhere up there ahead. Behind her suddenly she heard the lone howling of a wolf.

She had been watching a distant column of pale smoke rising in the air for some time before she realised what she was seeing. Her mind had been paralysed with exhaustion. Somewhere ahead someone had lit a fire.

She almost ran the last few hundred yards towards the shadowy buildings, dragging the horse behind her, and a dog started barking furiously. She could smell the scent of burning peat, sharp in the cold air.

The dim light of a candle appeared in a window and as she and the horse limped up the last of the track she heard the grating sound of a door being pulled open. Dimly she saw a hooded figure, a lanthorn in his hand, peering out of what must be the gatehouse to some lonely mountain homestead.

"Peace be with you, brother, you travel the pass late." A quiet voice challenged her out of the dark.

She was too tired even to check that her hair was concealed in her hood. "Please, give me shelter and food; my horse is lame. We were caught in the storm . . ." Her voice was husky and tearful as she pushed open the wooden gate and came to a halt in front of the man. In the light of his lanthorn she could see him more clearly now. He wore the unbleached woollen robe and cowl of a monk.

"Welcome, my brother." He took the reins from her hand. "Enter the guest-house and sit by the fire. I'll call someone to tend your beast and then I'll bring you food." He had a thin, lined face and sad grey eyes; there was no curiosity in his gaze, only concern as she half staggered through the door past him and found herself in a small stuffy room. Two candles burned by a simple prie-dieu in the corner and the peats glowed in the hearth. She sank shivering to her knees by the fire and held out her hands gratefully to the warmth.

The monk followed her in a few moments later. "I have sent for Brother Anselm," he said quietly. "He always looks after our injured beasts; he's tending a sick man at present, but I'm sure he'll be able to poultice your horse's leg. It's a fine animal." He was busying himself in the corner at a side table and she heard the clink of goblets.

When he brought her the mulled wine she was almost swaying with fatigue, but gratefully she took the goblet from him. The warmth spread quickly through her veins and she closed her eyes with a deep sigh.

With a start she realised the monk had been talking again: ". . . or would you rather sleep first?" She heard his voice through a haze and she jerked upright.

"I'm sorry?" she rubbed her face wearily with the back of her hand.

He gave a low chuckle. "Your weariness answers for you, child. Here, let me help you up. We have only one guest room, as it's not often we have visitors up here; but you shall have it. You can eat when you've slept."

His hand under her elbow was surprisingly firm as he led her through a low arched doorway into a passage. A few paces down it he threw open another door. His candle showed her a tiny little room furnished only with a bed and a stool. But the mattress was deep and the coarse homespun blankets looked warm and dry.

She didn't have the energy to pull off the wet torn buskins which clung so uncomfortably to her thighs. The last thing she remembered after the monk, with a soft *Benedicite*, had withdrawn, was throwing herself on the bed, dragging off the stiff damp hood and pulling the blankets up over her. Then all was darkness.

She slept for hours, the deep unconscious sleep of total exhaustion. When she woke it was full day. The small unshuttered window showed a grey cloudy sky and she shivered. She pulled herself to her feet and stretched wearily. Her clothes had dried on her and she felt warm, but her stomach griped with hunger. She listened at the door for a moment, tucking the tangled knot of hair at her neck into the top of her shirt. Then she eased it open and looked out. The passage was empty. She made her way uncertainly to the room where she had been given wine the night before. It too was deserted, but the goblets were still there, as was a jug of mead and a plate of cold bacon and coarse bread. The fire was out. She poured herself some mead and began to eat ravenously, breaking lumps off the hard bread and soaking them in the sweet liquid before she could bring herself to chew them.

Outside, through the unglazed windows, she could see the extent of the small community. The little church and cloisters stood on the far side of a muddy yard where a dozen or so hens pecked at the brown sodden grass. Somewhere she heard a horse whinny. There was a range of outbuildings roofed with turfs opposite the guest-house and in one she could see the outline of a figure wielding a pitchfork.

She jumped as the door near her opened and the monk came in. His grey face had been whipped to red across the cheekbones by the sharp wind.

"Good morning, child. I trust you slept well?" He rubbed his hands together to warm them and crossed to pour himself some mead. "Eat, my dear. I'll bring you some hot soup from the kitchen soon, when Brother Hugh gets the priory fires alight." He chuckled.

Isabel felt herself colouring nervously. "It's kind of you," she said uncertainly. "But, brother, I think you should know – I have no money to reward your charity."

"Nonsense," he laughed. "It wouldn't be charity if you paid for it, would it? Now, let me introduce myself. My name is Brother Aidan. I'm guest-master here; we sometimes have visitors when like yourself they're benighted at the head of the pass, but my job is not unduly hard, which is why Father Prior gives it to an old man like me." He smiled gently.

Isabel studied the tired, lined face and found herself smiling back. Instinctively she liked and trusted the old man. "Have I reached the pass then?" she asked eagerly. "I was so lost in that storm, I could only guess the direction."

"You're near it, aye."

"Brother, tell me the name of the pass. It may be the wrong one . . ." she hesitated as he refilled his goblet once again.

"They call it Lang Meikle," he said slowly over his shoulder. "It's the only road through for miles round here. In the summer people ride straight up over the Rig, but once the weather starts to break . . ." He shrugged. "The track goes round beneath the Rig about three miles up beyond the priory. The top of the pass is marked by an old stone cross, you can't miss it. Past it the road is clear. It drops very quickly down into the valley and then you'll find yourself following the Cannar Water south." He threw back his head and tipped the contents of the goblet down his throat.

"My horse, is he better?"

The monk shook his head. "I've been to see him. I'm afraid his leg is badly sprained. He can barely put his foot on the ground. Brother Anselm has bandaged it and given the horse restoratives, but," he shrugged, "it may be days before it is fit to travel." There was a moment's silence. Isabel's hopes had fallen and she stared blankly for a moment into the depths of her sweet golden drink.

When she looked up she found the old man's eyes on her. He had folded his arms, tucking his hands out of sight in the full sleeves of his robe.

"I saw despair in your face, sister," he said gently. "May I ask you how far you had hoped to travel?"

She felt her cheeks flame. "You knew I was a woman?"

Again he gave the comforting chuckle. "My eyes may be dim, my dear, and I may have been a long while in the service of God, but I'm not so decrepit that I can't recognise a maidenly curve when I see one. Now, you didn't answer my question."

She looked down. "I . . . I was trying to find a friend. We were supposed to be going to England together."

"Are you running away?"

The question, put so directly, took her aback. She began to stammer. "I . . . told you. I'm hoping to meet a friend. I got lost in the mountains last night and missed the path."

Agitated, she crossed to the window and looked out. "He was a day ahead of me. We were to meet at Lang

Meikle Rig." She had remembered the name with a little leap of excitement the moment the monk had spoken it. "I suppose he meant by the cross, I don't know for sure." She shrugged her shoulders in despair again. She had almost convinced herself that Andrew had never left Glencarnie alive; but even if he had, had Andrew ever given a thought to waiting for her, or had he turned north at once and taken a ferry back across the Forth?

She felt her eyes fill with tears. Behind her the old man busied himself with refilling her goblet. She heard the slap of his sandals on the flags as he brought it back to her. "Here, child, drink this. Now tell me, who were you hoping to meet?" His voice had become very gentle.

"Andrew Douglass. My betrothed." It wasn't really an untruth. Once she had considered him to be just that.

The old man rubbed his bony finger against his cheek. There was a troubled frown on his face. "Will you tell me your name, child?" he asked.

She told him and he shook his head sadly. "My dear, I have to tell you something. Come. Come and sit down." His strong arm round her shoulder guided her to a stool and pushed her gently down. "Yesterday our waggon picked up a young man on the hill track from the north. Two of our brothers were returning from the market."

She looked at him, her eyes blazing with excitement and hope. "Andrew? Was it Andrew?" she cried.

The monk slowly went to the hearth and kicked at the dead peats.

"He was very ill, my dear. Brother Columb found him lying in the heather with a bad head wound. They put him in the waggon and brought him home to our infirmary. Brother Anselm tended him as best he could, but he had a very high fever and he had lost a lot of blood." The old man paused as she rose, her heart thudding with fear, her face white.

"Where is he?"

"I'll take you to him, child. Come."

"Is he . . . will he recover?" The words came as a whisper as she followed Brother Aidan through the door.

He stopped abruptly and turned, his face full of compassion.

"I'm sorry. I thought you understood. He is with Christ, my child. He died just before prime, this morning, while you slept."

CHAPTER EIGHT

A PUDDLE of rippled brown water lay outside the guest-house and she stood staring down at it for a moment, stunned by his words. Andrew was dead. She would never again see those gentle grey eyes, hear his voice, feel his touch. He would never be able to help her find the king, to warn him, or take her to England where she could be safe from the Black Fox.

She felt a sudden illogical rush of anger that Andrew should let her down after all. She had not realised until that moment just how much she had counted on meeting him safely and leaving to him the urgent task of finding the king. Then she thought again of his kindness and loyalty to her and she found herself swallowing desperately, bitterly ashamed at her selfishness. She blinked hard, trying to hold back the rush of tears which threatened to come, and rubbed her sleeve across her eyes.

Brother Aidan had been watching her struggle. Sadly he nodded his head. "Would you rather not go to see him, child? It would upset you needlessly."

She shook her head dumbly and straightened her shoulders. "No. I want to see him. I must – I owe it to him. And besides –" she clutched suddenly at an impossible hope. "It might not be him. It could be another man . . ." But he shook his head again, and she knew there could be no doubt.

She followed him across the muddy yard to a small stone building at the far end of the cloisters. The room, as the door was pushed open, smelled strongly of the herbs burning in a brazier near the high bed.

Brother Aidan stepped back and let her enter alone. She stood and gazed down at the still figure on the bed. Candles burned at his head and feet and clasped in the hands folded on his breast was a carved wooden crucifix. His handsome face was smooth and cold as a marble effigy.

She couldn't stop the sob which rose in her throat as she looked down at him. It was her fault he was dead; her fault that he had left the north and ended up lying here in a tiny mountain priory, far from anyone he knew. With tears streaming down her face she took a step nearer to the bed. There was an ugly rugged scar across his temple half hidden by his hair, and blindly she bent and kissed it. Then she kissed his lips.

She heard Brother Aidan entering the room behind her, but she didn't look up.

"My child, he died thinking of you," he said softly. "Your name was on his lips. He wanted to return to fetch you from somewhere. He was very agitated in his fever about you. If I had only realised last night . " He shook his head slowly. "We never guessed you were following him, you see." He paused, then went on: "What will you do now?"

"I don't know." Her voice shook as she answered him. "I'm alone now; I don't know what to do."

She stood for a moment, her face streaked with tears, to look one last time at the man who had followed her and lost her, and then she crossed herself sadly, and turned to follow the old man out of the infirmary.

"I suppose I must carry on by myself," she said softly. "There's nothing else I can do now."

"To England?" He was concerned. "Can you not go home?"

She shook her head. "My father lives so far away, and besides he won't believe me. I have to warn someone . " She broke off suddenly, wondering if she could trust him, for whatever had happened, the king still had to be told of his danger. She could not forget her quest because Andrew could no longer help her. She must turn north and find the king and tell him that Duncan Crawfurd of Glencarnie was a traitor and a murderer.

There was no doubt in her mind how Andrew had died. Duncan had arranged to have him attacked and beaten.

He had lied to her and tricked her and thought to win her by deceit, and suddenly she was filled with hatred for the man.

She looked at the monk at her side and made up her mind to ask his help. "Brother Aidan, can I tell you the whole story? Even with Andrew dead," her voice faltered a little on the word, "I have to go on. I must find the king."

The old man's eyebrows shot up. "The king, lady? You'll not find him in England, I'm thinking."

She gave a watery smile. "Andrew and I had arranged to go to England before I learned about the king. I had to catch him up and then together we would have gone back – or perhaps have found messengers to send to him, I don't know." She took a deep breath and swallowed nervously. "I have just come from Glencarnie," she explained, trying to keep her voice steady. "I was affianced by the king to Sir Duncan Crawfurd although it was against my wishes, as I had already been long pledged to Andrew. Andrew came after me, to rescue me." She looked down at the ground, feeling the tears welling up again in her eyes. "We were captured almost at once, but somehow he escaped and as we had arranged to meet here if we were separated, I followed him south. He didn't know it, but before I left Glencarnie I overheard something which would have changed all our plans. Brother, I took an oath on the holy rood not to reveal what I am going to tell you, but my allegiance must absolve me from it, mustn't it?" She stopped anxiously, but he looked at her blankly, not understanding, so she plunged on. "They are planning to murder King James. And soon. That is why he must be warned somehow, before it's too late."

The monk paled visibly beneath his mountain tan. "Murder the king?" he repeated in disbelief.

"Yes. And I'm the only one who can warn him in time. Don't you understand? I've no reason to go on south now. I have to return north to find him – to Linlithgow, I suppose, if he's still there with the court."

She bit her lip. The road north would take her back

towards Glencarnie and now there was no Andrew to save her from the Black Fox if he should catch her again – and no reason for him to extend her any mercy once he had her in his hands.

Brother Aidan shook his head slowly. "Lady, this is all too much for me to understand. I must tell your story to our Father Prior. He will know what to do. Come. Wait in the guest-house while I go and speak to him. He is in the chapter-house at the moment, and maybe he will know how a message could be sent."

Gratefully she followed him back, her mind still numbed by what had happened. She had to concentrate on warning the king; that way she could shut from her mind the memory of that poor cold figure lying in the priory infirmary. It was so hard to realise that Andrew was truly dead. For so long she had carried his image with her, like an amulet. Andrew who could save her from Duncan; Andrew who could rescue her from Glencarnie; Andrew who would know at once how to reach the king. Andrew, who loved her.

She walked into the guest-house in a daze and sat down on the low stool, her hazel eyes blank with grief.

But had he really loved her? For a few brief moments she had wondered out there on the moor below Lady Rock whether he had only come out of a sense of loyalty and duty. Poor Andrew. If that were so his death seemed even more unjust and mean. Another little sob escaped her lips, for her own love for him, she had realised at that same moment really had been, as she had told Duncan, the love of a woman for a favourite brother and no more. Had it ever been anything else? She thought back to those long days and nights waiting for him to return from France. No, even then it had not been true love.

She refused to ask herself how she knew the difference suddenly between the two. That was a line of thought she would not and could not allow herself to pursue – not now that Duncan had shown himself to be a traitor and a murderer. She shrugged angrily. How had his name even crossed her mind at this moment when she was mourning someone as good and gentle as Andrew? She felt some-

thing wet on her hand and looked down surprised; she
hadn't realised that she was still crying.

The bell began tolling quietly from the little priory church
and she looked up at last. How long had she been sitting
there in the small cheerless room? She shivered, wish-
ing suddenly that she could light the fire, but there was
no sign of tinder or lights and no one to call to do it for
her.

   She got up heavily and walked to the doorway, wondering why Brother Aidan was taking so long to return to her.
She looked out. Beyond the priory wall she could see the
heavy clouds drifting down across the wet heather and
bracken, hiding the mountains and the sky alike in a
rolling wet mist. In the distance she could just see a small
figure running up the track towards the gates, a bundle of
sacking under its arm. She watched curiously as it drew
closer and the outline grew more distinct. It was a small
peasant boy, presumably from some neighbouring village.
To her surprise after climbing the gate and vaulting nimbly into the yard he ran straight towards her at the guest-
house door, where he stopped, panting.

   "Here's the kirtle, my lady," he piped, with a mis-
chievous grin. "Tell Brother Aidan it's the best my
mother had. She's right glad o' the siller pennies and she's
put a hood and her old cloak with it. She said it's gey
holey, but it'll serve tae keep the rain out." He thrust the
bundle at her and then with another cheeky grin he turned
and ran off again, leaping over the puddles.

   Isabel looked at the pile of old clothes in horrified
surprise. Then she understood and she blessed the old
man for his thoughtfulness in sending for woman's clothing for her. She had temporarily forgotten her discom-
fort, but it must have embarrassed him as much as herself
to see her in the tight-fitting breeches and buskins and the
crumpled shirt with its loose-laced neck.

   She took the bundle through into the little cell which
had been her bedroom the night before and unrolled it
gingerly.

   There was a kirtle of indigo-dyed homespun, a heavy

hodden hood and short cloak. All spotlessly clean, but shabby and mended. The woman who had sent the things must have been too poor to send a gown to wear over the kirtle; perhaps she didn't even own one, but what she had sent was more than welcome after the uncomfortable garments Isabel had been wearing for the last two days. She thankfully peeled them off one by one, leaving them lying crumpled on the bare floor. Then she pulled the kirtle over her head. Her benefactress was obviously a plump woman and not over tall. The bodice hung loosely over her breasts and the hem barely covered her ankles. She felt a ridiculous bitter giggle rising in her throat at the thought of what she must look like as she knotted the plaited girdle and pulled on the heavy shoes which had been tucked into the middle of the bundle. She braided her hair and pulled on the warm hood, flinching a little at its coarseness. Then she made her way back to the main room of the guest house. Brother Aidan had returned, and was kneeling before the fire, blowing at a small pile of smoking tinder.

"Thank you for the clothes," she murmured as she came to stand behind him. "That was thoughtful of you, brother. When may I see Father Prior?"

The old man looked up and for a moment he gazed at her solemnly. Then he nodded. "A woman in man's clothing is not pleasing to God, my child. I am glad they fit you."

He rose painfully to his feet, puffing slightly after his exertions with the fire.

"Father Prior is over busy this morning, child." He looked down suddenly, avoiding her eyes. "I have told him your story and he is truly sorry for your loss."

"But will he help me?" Isabel stared at the old man's drooping shoulders.

Brother Aidan shrugged. "There is little we can do. We are a poor community here, far from anywhere . . ."

"But surely, there is something you can do? Let me speak to the Prior, please, brother. I have to find the king. He must be warned quickly. Surely the Prior will know how to find the quickest way of reaching him?" She could hear her voice rising desperately as she spoke. She took a

step forward, gently putting her hand on his sleeve.
"Please, brother, you must help me."

Again the shrug. "Lady Isabel, you must know something. Sir Duncan Crawfurd of Glencarnie is our patron.
Father Prior dare not do anything to anger him. If he
withdrew his support . . ." He shrugged again as she
gasped.

"You mean he won't help?"

"He daren't, my lady."

She turned and dropped on to the stool. "So, rather
than antagonise Sir Duncan your Prior would risk his
king's life!" She could feel her hands beginning to
shake.

The old man raised his eyes from the floor at last. He
looked at her miserably. "We have no choice, little sister.
We are a poor foundation, without Sir Duncan we would
cease to exist. Don't you see?"

She rose. "Oh yes, I see. I see very well." She picked up
the rough unbleached cloak and flung it around her shoulders. "It seems it is up to me alone then. As my horse is
lame, perhaps you would let me take Andrew's. I must
ride to find the king alone."

He looked anxious. "Sister, please stay. Wait. I'll go
and speak to the Prior again."

"No, I must go now." She was driven by deep despair
and disappointment. There was no reason to wait, no one
to look for, nowhere to go, save to the king and then with
his mercy and blessing back to Strathblair. Alone.

"Tell someone to saddle the horse for me."

Again he shook his head. "Lady, there is no horse," he
said gently.

"No horse?" She swung round, her eyes narrowed suddenly in disbelief.

"No, my lady. I told you. Your Andrew was found lying
in the heather at the roadside. The brothers who found
him thought he was either thrown by his horse which then
must have bolted, or he was attacked and the animal
stolen. There was no horse there."

For a moment she was defeated, and the mention of
Andrew's name brought fresh tears, still so near the sur-

face, back to her eyes, but she dashed them away with the back of her hand.

"Very well, then I must take one of your horses. You shall keep mine in exchange."

He gave a slow smile. "We have but one horse here and he is scarcely a fit exchange for yours, lady. No, there is nothing for it but to stay." He walked stiffly towards the side table and reached inevitably once again for the jug. "Here, take a sup of mead, my lady. It will restore you. Then later perhaps I can approach the father again."

She took the mug from him and sipped the honeyed sweetness of the mead. It warmed her, flowing comfortingly through her veins, and for a moment she was tempted to do as he suggested. Stay; rest; let it pass; let others worry; the king's guards surely would protect him from any danger. Her safest course would be to rest until the horse was mended and then ride south to England, far from the Black Fox's clutches.

She could feel Brother Aidan's gaze on her, watching her anxiously for her decision. Was it her imagination or was he looking ashamed and apprehensive now? A sudden suspicion dawned in her mind. What was there to stop the prior sending a message to Duncan telling him that she was here? Perhaps he had already done it. What better way to curry favour with their powerful patron?

She set down the mug abruptly. "No, brother, thank you. I daren't delay. Duncan," she broke off quickly – "the plotters must by now know that I have run away and they will have guessed that I know their plans. They may even now be following me. I must ride on. I'll take your horse; perhaps I can get a better at the nearest burgh. Please." She put her hands in his impulsively. "You must see how important this is. Don't tell Father Prior you have let me go. He told you to keep me here, didn't he?" She looked at him earnestly and saw at once the unhappy blush which coloured the old man's cheeks. In spite of the bolt of fear which shot through her she smiled at him. "Hurry, brother; show me the horse, and I shall steal it when you're not looking."

He hurried after her as she pushed through the door out

into the mizzling rain. The barn door hung half open and she slipped through it and stopped, trying to accustom her eyes to the gloom. The chestnut was tethered in one corner, its head hanging listlessly, its off foreleg bandaged from knee to hoof. Tied to a ring near it was an aged bay horse with a staring coat and protruding ribs.

The monk who had followed her in smiled ruefully. "Poor Bayard has seen better days. He's of an age to retire, lady, not gallop the hills in the mist." He ran a gentle hand over the animal's bony back. "We haven't a saddle for him and yours won't fit the poor beast." He eyed the ornate leather saddle which was lying over one of the low beams which divided the barn down the centre.

"Then I must ride bareback. He has a bridle, I take it?" She was becoming impatient with the old man's stalling. Every second counted.

The monk lifted it down from a hook and fitted it gently over the horse's halter. It had long driving reins.

She scrambled on to the horse's back from one of the beams and arranging her skirts as best she could she gathered up the reins. "Thank you, brother. You have been kind." She hesitated a moment, looking down at his gentle upturned face. "Pray for me – please."

He patted the horse's neck. "I will, little sister, I will. There is one thing . . ." he hesitated, his hand still clasping the rein. "Father Prior forbade me to tell you this, but already my disobedience is great, and I too am loyal to the crown." He shrugged philosophically. "It appears that the king is actually here in these hills. He is hunting from Craig Law Castle. If you follow the road south over the pass and seek directions when you reach Cannar you may find him. Now, go, and God go with you, child."

"Bless you, brother, for telling me that." She gave him a grateful smile. "I hope you won't get into trouble with your superior. Blame me for everything." She slapped the horse's neck with the rein and urged it out of the barn, leaving the old man gazing after her from the doorway.

The horse had an uncomfortable rolling gait and twice she nearly tumbled from its back as they turned southwards down the track. Then, her hand firmly entwined in its mane, she settled to its stride and set about urging it as fast as she could up the hill towards the head of the pass.

All round her the low clouds drifted in white mist, enveloping her in a cold wet world where she could see but a few feet in front. She pulled the cloak more tightly round her and peered nervously ahead, riding as fast as she dared, putting as much distance as she could between herself and the priory, every second expecting to hear sounds of pursuit.

The track began to climb more steeply as it approached the summit, and she allowed the old horse to slow to a walk. It was blowing badly, shaking its head with indignation at being made to gallop after so many years plodding before the plough. Over the pass, several miles further on, she would come to the little market town of Cannar in the broad river glen where she hoped she would be able to beg, or even steal, a fresh horse and find news of the king.

"Not far, Bayard, not far," she whispered in the animal's ear and she saw it flicker for an instant in response.

Then before she had expected it she found herself at the head of the pass. Above her the mist thinned imperceptibly and she could see thin traces of blue sky; below the thick clouds billowed and writhed in a slight wind, filling the valley with chill cloying mist.

She reined in and looked round with a little lift of the spirits at the sight of the sky; if only the mist would clear. Bayard raised his head sharply and whinnied; a long, piercing call, vibrating through his whole body. Shaken, she hushed him, glancing behind, and then she too heard the other horse.

For a moment she sat still, listening to the muffled thunder of the hooves on the track behind her, then panic seized her. Why should anyone be riding so fast, at full gallop, breakneck speed in the thick mist, unless they were in pursuit of something – or someone?

Vainly she tried to beat Bayard into a gallop with a stick but the animal was exhausted. He could scarcely shamble into a trot. She turned, her heart in her mouth, and saw in the hazy distance the black horse appear suddenly on the ridge, its rider bending low over its neck; it was coming at full gallop up the track and within seconds it would over-take her.

She reined in her horse herself and waited, shaking, her eyes fixed on the spiky black mane which her fingers were still clutching so convulsively. She did not have to raise her eyes to identify the rider.

Duncan's horse reared, snorting, as he pulled it savagely to a halt.

"Once again I have to gallop half across Scotland to catch you, my lady." His voice was harsh. "May I ask where you intended going this time?"

"To the king." She looked up at him defiantly.

His hard face was set in an uncompromising scowl. "The king! To beg him to release you from our betrothal? Do you really think he would?"

"Yes, I think he would." A cloud drifted up towards them from the corrie below and they were enclosed in the thick white world again. Rain began to fall, chilling their faces, dripping from the horses' necks. Duncan's stallion shook its head impatiently and a shower of droplets flew.

"He would release me from any vow made to you." She put every ounce of disdain she could into her voice, for what had she to lose now?

He raised an eyebrow. "So, the death of the faithful swain has goaded you to more desperate measures. When the priory messenger met me this morning and said that you and he were there I thought for a moment he'd returned to try and rescue you. But I find that after all he'd fled alone. How inconvenient that he should have died before you could catch up with him."

"Don't dare to speak of Andrew like that!" she flashed at him furiously. "He was a good and loyal friend. He loved me and he loved his king."

She was terrified of Duncan but suddenly her anger and indignation at his treachery were stronger than her fear. "Andrew was a fine man. Had he known what you were planning he would have killed you with his bare hands when he had the chance."

He looked down at her, his face impassive for a

moment. "And what, pray, besides marrying you, am I supposed to be contemplating which would rouse the inestimable Andrew to such fury?"

"Murder!"

She hissed the word at him. She knew at once she had made a mistake as his face contorted with anger. He swung down from his horse and strode to her side, his hand descending in an iron grip on her wrist where her fingers still clutched the bay's black mane. So he hadn't known about her discovery. He had set out in pursuit of her without realising that she had overheard the plan and after all Margaret had not betrayed her. But it was too late to take the word back. He had heard it and he knew.

"What did you say?" His voice was cold as ice.

"I said murder. I know all about it, so don't deny it." She rushed on recklessly, not caring now what she said. "You plan to kill King James; you are a traitor and a murderer!" Her own eyes were blazing with fury as she tried to free her wrist from his grip.

"Who told you?" he asked suddenly.

"Nobody told me. I heard you. You and your precious friends; don't you remember? You were about to marry me, then you had to send me away for a secret conference. Well, you didn't close the door properly behind you and I heard every word!"

"You stupid little bitch!" He didn't slacken his grip. "You could have ruined everything. Who have you told about this? Who?" He shook her arm furiously.

"No one, except the monk who cared for me." She was shocked into telling him the truth. "He told the Prior, but they didn't believe me. And they betrayed me in sending a message to you," she added bitterly.

He ignored her last remark. "You told them that I was involved?"

She swallowed and looked away suddenly. "Well, not you. I just said that the plotters were from Glencarnie."

Angrily, he slammed his hand down against his thigh. "That's enough to betray us. You foolish girl; why couldn't you have minded your own business?"

"It is my business, Sir Duncan." She managed somehow to keep her voice level. "You were intending to marry me at the same moment you were planning the murder of a king!"

She had a sudden vision of King James at Linlithgow, his hand on her arm, whispering to her about Duncan: "He's a handsome young man . . . and not unkind . . ." and then, "Remember, I am your friend . . ." She felt very sick. "What did you intend doing with me? After King James had died I suppose you'd have murdered me too. What point was there to your agreement with the king then? Marry me hastily to reassure the king of your obedience and then what?" she cried. "Take me to court to show him your dutiful wife and stick a sword into his heart?"

"God damn it, Isabel, be silent!" He released her wrist suddenly. "It was not going to be like that at all." The wind stirred his black riding cloak. "I would never have harmed you. But now you know too much; far too much."

For one moment she met his eyes as he looked up at her. They were cold and calculating, hard as steel. Terror clutched at her throat.

Instinctively she acted. She raised her arm with its stick and brought it down hard across his unprotected, upturned face. He staggered back, his hands to his eyes, as she wheeled Bayard round and sent him thundering down the track, praying that the mist would be thick enough to hide her before Duncan had a chance to recover. There was no sound from behind, only the gentle moaning of the wind and the steady drumming of her own horse's hooves.

Bayard began to wheeze uncomfortably almost at once, but somehow she forced him on, cutting unmercifully at his rump with the stick. Once across the the bare flat ground at the top of the pass the mist was heavier again and she plunged into it, allowing the horse to slow to a trot. Then she turned him sharply off the track to the left down the slope. Some trees were growing there in a small glen, their branches floating disembodied in the milky whiteness. She guided the exhausted horse into it and slid to the ground.

Holding her breath, she listened. There was no sound

from the track behind her. The mist drifted a little, thinning then thickening, amongst the trees. She could feel a sob of terror in her throat as she stood, her hand on the horse's muzzle. It was quite silent. The mist muffled the sound of the dripping trees and the horse's heavy breathing, and there was no sound from the heather and bracken on the slope. Isabel stroked the horse's head gently. Her hand was shaking violently and her heart beat so loudly that she felt sure he must be able to hear it.

Bayard shook his head impatiently, rattling the bit against his teeth, and she froze, closing her eyes tightly for a moment. When she opened them she thought the mist had cleared slightly. Everywhere the silence pressed against her eardrums and she could picture Duncan somewhere out there on the hillside listening for her.

She turned and very cautiously glanced round. As far as she could see the hillside rose steeply behind her; the water dripped dankly from the shiny areas of stark rock and it was thick with ferns and clinging grasses. A breath of wind stirred the mist and she saw a darker shadow on the face of the rock. Was it a cave? Looking back at the horse she made a quick decision. Cautiously turning the animal, she knotted the reins around its neck.

"Go home, Bayard," she whispered. "Go home and take him after you." Then she thwacked the horse on the rump. It threw up its head, startled, and crashed up the bank behind her. There it stopped, its ears laid back against its head.

"Oh, go; please go," she breathed, not daring to move. "Go on, or you'll bring him straight here. Please go on." She was clenching her fists until her nails bit into the palms of her hands. The horse gave a little whicker and began to trot forward purposefully. In a moment it had vanished into the mist.

She waited without moving, holding her breath. Then slowly she began to pick her way carefully up towards the steep hillside which backed the corrie ahead of her. A twig broke beneath her shoe and she stopped dead, holding her breath again. Then cautiously she crept on, thankful that she wasn't hampered by the long full skirts and train of a

gown. Her short peasant's kirtle made it much easier for
her to scramble, pulling herself up with the help of ivy
roots and tussocks of the coarse wild grasses.

After only ten minutes' climbing she was shaking with
exhaustion and strain. She rubbed the back of her hand
across her eyes and stopped for a moment to gather her
strength. She longed to throw off the heavy hood but she
dared not release her precarious handhold. "Only a few
minutes," she breathed to herself. "I must be nearly
there." She glanced up. The shiny rock face she had
noticed from the ground was just above her and to the
right. She swung herself towards it, her feet scrambling
desperately for footholds on the slippery surface. Around
her the mist was thinning. Higher up above the rock a tree
suddenly emerged, bathed in strange hazy sunlight.

Then she was there. She looked round for the cave
entrance. Where was it? Surely she had not mistaken the
direction. Frantically she scrambled further along the
rock. Then she saw it. The rock opened out into a shallow
hollow, not more, now that she was near enough to see,
than four feet deep, open-mouthed and quite unsheltered
save for a few clumps of willow-herb and toadflax which
waved gently in the breeze.

She pulled herself up on to the ledge and crouched
there, panting, as the first shafts of sunlight pierced
through the mist near her and lit her refuge as clearly as
the blazing candelabra lit the mummers on a stage.

She shrank back as best she could, thankful for the dull
unbleached grey-brown of her cloak and hood, watching
the ground appear beneath her – first the tree-tops, then
the bank, and then the empty moorland, stretching
towards the haziness which was the horizon.

She strained her eyes into the distance, looking for
either of the horses, the ragged bay or the great shiny
black, but the countryside seemed deserted as far as she
could see, and with a sigh of relief she sat back on her heels
and rested her head for a moment on her arms, trying to
recover her breath before she looked again. Somewhere in
the distance she could hear the liquid falling note of the
curlew.

There was a sharp crack immediately below her. She looked down, her heart beating, straining her eyes through the russet canopy of leaves. Nothing moved. She edged forward slightly to peer over the lip of the ledge.

The black stallion was tethered to a bush almost immediately beneath her. Her hand flew to her lips to stifle a cry of fright which almost betrayed her while her eyes frantically scoured the trees for a sign of Duncan. There was no sound, and even as she watched the horse relaxed, slack at the hip, and lowered its head to nibble at the lush woodland grass.

She glanced up. There was no escape that way. The cliff became sheer above her head. Further on to the right a tiny brown burn tumbled precipitously from its crevice source in the slippery rock, losing itself in spray long before it hit the ground. Her refuge had become a trap from which there was only one way in or out.

Cautiously she began to edge back the way she had come along the cliff, away from the grazing horse, pressing herself against the grass as close as she could, her nails tearing as she groped for handholds amongst the rocky soil and leaves. If she could get beyond the next bank of trees she would be hidden from the clearing where the horse grazed. Her breath was rasping in her throat with the effort and for the hundredth time she had to fling a handhold aside in order to pull the dragging kirtle away from a tree root. She looked back. The horse still stood unconcerned.

In another moment she would reach the sheltering overhang of trees with their curtaining ivy. She reached out and pulled herself in amongst them and then rested for a moment, gasping for breath. All was silent below her.

As quickly as she could she lowered herself until she was once more on the thick carpet of dead leaves. She glanced round and then started to run blindly through the copse. The trees grew thickly here, tangled and knotted with brambles, cutting off her escape. Almost at her feet a blackbird suddenly flew up with a deafening staccato scream. She put her hands to her head in panic and whirled about, lost, seeing for the first time how the blood trickled down her arm where she had snagged it on a sharp twig.

"I think that's far enough, don't you?" The cool voice spoke only yards from her. With a sharp cry she swung round.

He was sitting, arms folded, on a fallen tree-trunk at the far side of a small clearing. Before him the whole cliff rose clearly, flooded with the cold sunlight. He must have been able to watch her every move from his seat.

There was a dangerous smile on his lips as he rose to his feet and stepped towards her. "I think this comedy has gone on long enough, Isabel," he said quietly.

She backed away from him until she was brought up short by a tangle of hazel and aspen boughs.

In a moment his hands were on her shoulders and he was dragging her back with him into the centre of the sunlit clearing.

"I intend to settle this business once and for all," he growled, his face only inches from hers. "And when I've finished with you, Isabel Douglass, you'll think no more about betraying me to the king, that I promise you."

CHAPTER
NINE

SHE shrank away from him with a gasp of terror, but his grip was unrelenting and automatically she raised her hands towards his face, ready to rake her nails, her only weapon now, across his features. Then she stopped, appalled, as she saw a long double bruise across his forehead and the bridge of his nose. Seeing the direction of her horrified gaze he gave a short sharp laugh.

"Yes, you did that, my tender love. Do you intend to add to my wounds?" and his hand reached up to catch her wrists.

For a moment they stood there, looking at each other without speaking, and then, with an oath, he pulled her to him and drew her against his chest, pressing his burning lips against hers. For a moment she struggled, then slowly, her head reeling, she felt herself grow limp and helpless in his arms as once more the small fiery quivers of excitement began to whisper treacherously through her limbs.

They stood together for a long time in that clearing in the trees. Unnoticed by either of them the hazy sunlight vanished and slowly the mist began to reform in the secret hollow places of the wood, drifting across the face of the cliff as the imperceptible wind brought in more low, drifting clouds which slowly hid the distant hills and crags again.

When at last he released her she was breathless and shaking. She looked up into his face, dazed.

"I don't understand," she murmured. "I thought you wanted to kill me."

She saw the familiar gold glints appear at the corners of his eyes. "I may have done on several occasions," he chuckled softly, "I probably still should. You deserve it after the dance you've led me, vixen."

He raised his hands to her head and pulled off the hood, allowing the two heavy braids to fall down her back, the black hair like midnight silk against the coarse pale homespun. Then he kissed her again.

But already she was pushing him away. Her whole body tingled from his touch but she was still troubled and angry.

"What about the king?" she asked stubbornly. "It's not true, is it? I misunderstood what I heard?"

All the tenderness vanished from his face. It was suddenly black with anger and she shrank from him. Turning from her he reached up and grabbed at the dangling branch of an aspen, snapping it with his hands in a gesture of furious helplessness. "You did not misunderstand," he said harshly. "I am pledged to kill King James." He swung round. "You must try and trust me, Isabel. I know it's hard, but I beg you to trust me. I know what I'm doing."

Her face had gone white beneath the streaks of mud which unknowingly she'd rubbed across her cheeks.

"You can't know what you're doing. To kill a king? He's anointed before God!"

"He's chosen by man, Isabel. There are many who dispute the right of that branch of the Stewart family to rule this country, many who think of him as a tyrant, many who resent the large fortune in ransom money that's been paid to the English on his behalf. Oh, no, there are many who deny your reasoning and say that James Stewart must die. Listen, sweetheart," he stepped forward, taking her hands before she could dodge out of reach. "Forget about the king. Leave him to me. I'll not forget that he has done me one good turn at least. I admit that I had no wish for your hand when he forced it on me to check my quarrel with your father, and I planned to postpone the wedding until, well, until the king would be in no position to force anything on me against my wishes. But then I saw you, and I knew that I wanted you. You were the woman for the Black Fox. No other would do, in spite of your tainted Douglass blood and your wilful ways!" He laughed as with a furious gasp of indignation she tried to free herself from his grasp. "Your spirit fascinated me, sweetheart. You are the perfect mate for a man such as I."

For a moment she was speechless at his arrogance, and then she managed a retort. "You mean for someone brutal and violent and wild," she cried desperately, trying to free herself.

"Just so." He laughed again.

"And what about Margaret?" she flashed. "The beautiful Lady Margaret! Isn't she wilful too? Doesn't she share your characteristics – as well as your bed?" As she flung the accusation at him she felt herself colouring slightly.

He chuckled, not the least bit embarrassed. "Oh, I admit that I have passed the time of day with Margaret. She's beautiful and she's wild, yes. But I've never loved her."

"She claims you promised to marry her."

"She may have hoped so, my love, but she never heard any such promise from my lips. Was that why she was so anxious to help you escape my clutches?" He grinned at her guilty gasp.

"Did she tell you that herself?"

"She wouldn't have dared. No, that was my cousin Malcolm. He was so incensed that you were allowed to make off with his chestnut jade, never mind his precious breeks, that he told all!" He threw back his head and roared with laughter as she felt her cheeks become a fiery red. Then at once he was serious again. He held her at arms' length, compelling her to look at him. "Listen, I can tell you this much about Margaret. She has been useful to me. It was through her that I met certain lords who are with me in our enterprise against the king. Her brother is one of the leaders. It was imperative that I keep Margaret well-disposed and then he would join our plans. That is all. I care not a fig for her, I swear it. And her attitude to you –" he eyed her speculatively, "– although it hasn't surprised me, has not further endeared her to me, I assure you."

She lowered her eyes before the intensity of his gaze. "It didn't seem that way to me."

"Oh, indeed. And are you so experienced in the ways of

the world that you can guess at a man's heart as soon as look at him? I don't think so, in spite of your experience with the faithful Andrew."

She drew away from him abruptly at the mention of the name, her face betraying transparently her sudden misery, and he cursed himself silently for his lack of tact. Even more so when she turned on him suddenly.

"How *did* he escape from Glencarnie, sir?" she asked him, her hazel eyes holding his.

He looked uncomfortable. "If you must know, sweetheart, I ordered it. The Black Fox grows soft in his old age – that's what my men will say of me – but when you told me you loved him as a brother you yourself saved his life. I would not have let him live, had he been my rival. And had I known he would make at once for a prearranged meeting place with you I might not have been so generous." He smiled wryly. "But as it was, I thought of him as your brother and I remembered the sacrifice you were prepared to make for your other brother, little Ian, and, well," he shrugged, "I knew you would never have forgiven me had I caused his death. So I let him go."

She wanted to believe him, but still at the back of her mind there hovered the one thing which made her uncertain. "But he died," she said quietly.

"Aye, he died, and I'm truly sorry for that, Isabel. The men who attacked him will be caught and punished, that I promise you. I swear his death had nothing to do with me. Why should it? I could have killed him a dozen times within my own castle – I had no need to have him murdered beyond my gates."

He looked at her with such sincerity that she was overwhelmed with a quick rush of relief.

But already his expression was changing. The kindness had gone. In its place the old mocking mask was back. "Come, the mist is coming up again and I want a roof over my head tonight. What became of that strange misbegotten creature you were riding?"

In spite of herself Isabel felt her lips trembling into a smile. "He's well on his way home, I trust, if he has the strength."

He nodded. "Good. Then you shall ride with me on Thane." He took her arm. "We'll make for Cairn Dyke tonight. A cousin of mine lives there. Then in the morning I shall find someone to see you safe back to Glencarnie while I attend to matters elsewhere."

She froze. "What matters?"

He looked at her angrily. "That's my business, madam."

"Not the murder. Oh please, not the murder."

For a moment he stopped and swung to face her. "Isabel, I warn you. You are not to think about it. What I do does not concern you in any way. If I don't think I can trust you, I'll have my cousin Donald throw you in his dungeons until the whole business is over. I don't intend to let you jeopardize my plans."

She did not doubt his word for a moment. She was amazed at the speed with which he could change from a passionate lover to a ruthless stranger, and she shivered.

He led her to the place where his stallion was tethered. Gathering up the reins he threw her up behind the saddle and then vaulted on himself, setting the horse at a canter up the steep bank so that Isabel had to cling round his waist to keep her balance, and she found herself very conscious of the strong masculine feel of him and of the iron-hard muscles of his back beneath her cheek.

He cut across the moor towards the west, ignoring the path, heading for a distant vee-shaped pass between two of the highest peaks, barely visible in the mist. Darkness was drifting in behind them with the murk and night was already approaching.

"We're lucky we're near Donald's house," he shouted back over his shoulder after a while. "I'll warrant that you're tired, and I could do with a flagon of small beer myself."

The horse didn't falter as he set it at the rising ground, but it was nearly full dark before they saw the black shape of the tower house of Cairn Dyke rising in silhouette against the last streaks of green in the western sky. Duncan rode up to the high walls and yelled up at the battlements, his hands cupped around his mouth. There was no moat, no outer wall, only the high tower house itself with, suddenly appearing, the light of a brazier behind the battlements.

"Who goes?" The echoing call of the watchman came to them through the night.

"Tell Donald Fleming that the Black Fox demands a night's lodging from him," Duncan shouted back, his voice echoing in the misty silence.

Isabel saw the tall figure of a man stand upright on the battlement for a moment, silhouetted before his fire. Then, one hand raised in acknowledgement, he disappeared.

The black stallion stamped impatiently in the cold as they waited in the dark and Duncan put his hand restlessly on the hilt of his sword.

It was several minutes before anything happened. Then a faint, flickering light appeared in one of the lower windows.

"Suspicious fool," Duncan burst out. "He thinks I lead a raiding party." He spurred the horse up to the heavy studded door and drawing his sword he beat on it with the hilt.

"It's I, Duncan Crawfuru; alone with no one but a woman to hinder me. Open up, in the name of pity!" And again he thundered on the door.

Only after a long delay was it at last dragged open, and three men appeared on the threshold, carrying flaming torches.

"Aye, so it is you indeed, Black Fox," the man at the centre of the trio roared out. "Welcome, cousin, welcome." He strode forward as Duncan slipped from the horse and lifted Isabel to the ground.

"We're benighted, old friend." Duncan clapped the man on the shoulder. "Come on, let us inside. I'd rather that door of yours was between us and the bare hillside, though I doubt if you'll have raiders on a night like this."

Donald threw back his head and laughed. "I do all the raiding round here these days. You should see how my cattle herds increase!" He led the way in and Duncan

followed, holding Isabel's arm. The great black horse
followed meekly behind them, ducking its head under the
stone arch. Then the door was slammed to, and a battery
of bolts were thrown across to secure it. Instantly they
were surrounded by the warm friendly smell of horses.

"My man will bed down your beast. We've a spare stall
over there. Now, come you up to the fire, and your lassie
there with you." Donald's face in the light of the flickering
flame was ruddy and good-natured, but it had been badly
disfigured by an ugly purple scar which ran diagonally
across his face from temple to chin.

He led them by way of a steep corner staircase into a
crowded noisy hall. His wife still sat there at the table
amongst the remains of an evening meal and as Isabel and
Duncan followed Donald up to the dais she hospitably
made room for Isabel at her side.

"It is lucky that Donald was not back from the hunt till
after dark. We've hot food and plenty to spare. Make
yourself at home, lady." She smiled shyly. She was a thin,
colourless girl in her early twenties, Isabel guessed, and
obviously the robust Donald's second wife, for he presented Isabel a minute later to his two strapping sons who
towered above their stepmother and seemed more than
her equal in age.

Isabel saw Meg Fleming eyeing her strange garb curiously, but the girl was too well-mannered to comment.
Instead she called for food, and Isabel found herself sitting
before a plate of hot savoury stew which gave off a
mouth-watering smell of herbs and wine, as Donald himself cut off a trencher of bread with his knife and put it
beside her place. She glanced at Duncan. He too had been
given food, but he seemed more interested in the brim-
ming wooden quaich which had been passed to him.
Throwing back his head he drained it in one gulp and held
it out to be refilled. This time he paused and raised it
towards his hostess. "Here's a toast, my friends. To our
fair ladies, your lovely Meg and my Isabel."

Isabel looked down, blushing.

"Aye, and here's another." Donald rose to his feet. "To
King Jamie, God bless him."

"King Jamie." Duncan echoed the toast and Isabel saw him give her a long glance. She pushed her spoon doggedly into the bowl and refused to meet his eye.

In spite of the heat in the noisy hall she had found that her exhaustion had vanished. As she ate her mind was busy. Somehow she had to get a message to Donald. He might be Duncan's cousin but he was also the king's man – his loyal toast had proved that – and he would know if there were a way of warning the king – and of stopping Duncan. She frowned absently, nibbling at the hunk of bread, as she tried to put out of her mind the memory of Duncan's kiss. He had asked her to trust him, and her whole being ached to do so, but she dared not. She could not risk the life of the king if it were in her power to save him.

She glanced round the table. The men were beginning to thump the handles of their knives on the cloth in time to the lively tune being scraped out on a fiddle somewhere down in the body of the hall. The atmosphere grew hotter and more close and again the wineskin was passed round. She became conscious that Donald was once again leaning across to Duncan and imperceptibly she edged sideways to hear what was said.

"Are you joining the king's hunting party, my friend?"

Isabel tensed as Duncan, leaning lazily back in his chair, smiled down at the table, helping himself to a costard apple from a bowl.

"Which hunting party is this, coz? I've no desire to ride back to Linlithgow this side of Christmas. The king kept me there too long on my last visit."

"Not Linlithgow. The king is here at Craig Law, not a dozen miles from here. I'm going over there tomorrow myself. Come with me – there'll be good sport if this accursed mist rises."

Duncan closed his eyes for a moment, seeming to consider. When he opened them he was looking straight at Isabel. She could feel her cheeks reddening and she swallowed hard. He had seen her listening. Her mind raced. The king was close at hand; Donald was going there tomorrow. Somehow she must get a message to him without delay. But how? How could she warn him – without implicating Duncan?

She glanced down at her plate as she thought again of the passion of Duncan's kisses, and her body burned at the memory. She was torn first one way and then the other, first by her loyalty to the king and then by the strength of the strange emotions which gripped her. Surely it couldn't be that she was falling in love with this dark savage man whom she hated and feared. She glanced at him again under her eyelashes and blushed as she found that he was still watching her intently. She wondered if he could guess what was going on in her mind. Defiantly she held his gaze and she saw a mocking smile touch his lips as she looked away from him.

"Do you wish for fruit, my lady?" Meg was holding the apple bowl out to her. She took an apple absently, rubbing the shiny ribbed skin between her fingers and thumb and smiling at the serene face before her.

At that moment the idea came to her. She would confide in Meg. She was bound to get the chance to talk to her hostess alone and then the woman could pass the message to her husband later in the privacy of their own chamber. Isabel's relief at so simply solving her main problem was so great that she found herself giving the startled girl a brilliant smile as she bit into the apple. She refused even to look at Duncan again. His cousin could have the problem of how to warn the king. She would leave it to him to decide how to do it.

It was not long afterwards that Meg rose and led the way to the women's quarters. Isabel found she was to share a chamber with three other women, for space was limited in the restricted confines of the tower, but after her tiring day she was relieved to find there was any kind of a bed at all She eyed it longingly as Meg bade her goodnight, conscious of the other women listening and staring curiously at her clothes, but she couldn't go to sleep yet. As Meg turned to go she grabbed desperately at her hand. "Please, I must speak to you," she whispered urgently. "Is there somewhere we can be alone?"

Meg frowned, but without argument she led Isabel through another crowded chamber into a small oratory built into the thickness of the wall. She crossed herself piously in the light of the two candles burning before the statue of the Virgin and then turned to face Isabel enquiringly.

"What is it, my lady? You seem troubled." Her calm face was gently sympathetic.

Isabel glanced cautiously over her shoulder. They had left Duncan embarking with his host on yet another jug of wine, and yet somehow she had the feeling that at any moment he might appear in the low doorway behind her.

"You must ask your husband to take a message to the king," she whispered. "It is very urgent. An attempt is to be made on his life by some of those closest to him. It might even be tomorrow. I don't know. But please, please see that he is warned."

She pulled the homespun cloak closer round her shoulders as a draught from somewhere stirred the candle flames on the altar.

Meg stared at her, her mouth open. "Are you sure?" She looked disbelieving. "How do you know?"

"Never mind how I know, that's not important. But I am sure. You must get the message through, and please," she hesitated, trying to gauge the other woman's feelings, "please, tell him not to say a word to Sir Duncan about it."

Meg's eyes widened. "Sir Duncan? You can't mean . . ."

"I don't mean anything. I would just rather he didn't mention it. Please." It wasn't what she had meant to say. She had wanted to beg them to stop Duncan; to save him from his own folly, but she couldn't now. She waited, holding her breath as the other woman stared at her for a moment in silence. Then slowly her hostess nodded.

"I'll see the message gets there, my lady, don't fret yourself. Donald will warn him tomorrow before the hunt. Now, away to your bed and rest. I'll have new clothes laid out for you in the morning." She still had not enquired why the Lady Isabel Douglass of Strathblair was riding round the country dressed in the clothes of the meanest peasant, and Isabel did not feel like explaining. She was too tired.

Gratefully she squeezed Meg's hand and then, overcome at last with exhaustion, she went back to find her bed, peeling off the heavy damp dress before she crawled, aching with tiredness, between the covers.

She had meant to try and save Duncan. She did not want him to pay the penalty of his plan – too many people had died already. But what could she do to stop him? Miserably she closed her eyes. Her love for him, if love it was, had been doomed from the start, as had any she had felt for Andrew. Poor Andrew. At the thought of him, alone on his monastic bier in the lonely priory on the pass, she felt the tears of loneliness and misery begin to trickle down her cheeks once more and she turned her face into the pillow and wept silently.

Isabel was awakened at dawn by the other girls in the high chamber giggling and chattering as they dressed. It was very cold in the room, for the window was unshuttered and unglazed and the white mist was drifting round the embrasure leaving the stone glistening with moisture. Isabel slipped on the spotless shift and kirtle which she found laid on the chest at the end of the bed. Then she was helped by a cheerful red-headed girl to put on the fullskirted gown of palest woad-dyed soft wool. The girl did the lacing for her and helped her braid her hair before turning to her own toilet. On the chest there was also a fur-lined mantle which gratefully she pulled round her shoulders before she went to the window to look out. The world was once again white in the drifting mist, tinged here and there with pink from the rising sun. She could smell the resin from the fir trees whose topmost fronds she could just see emerging from the mist beyond the tower.

Duncan was awaiting her in the hall where a quick breakfast of bread and pasties was set on the long table.

"Good morning, Sir Duncan," she greeted him demurely, not daring to raise her eyes to his. She accepted a mug of thin ale from a page and then at last glanced up at Duncan's face. It was impassive.

"You slept well, I trust?" he asked her.

She nodded. "And you?"

"And I. Thank you. We'll leave at once after you've eaten. I find I have to go back to Glencarnie at once."

"Are we going straight there?" She tried to sound casual as she helped herself to one of the hot spiced pasties.

"Straight there, my lady. Both of us." His glance was instantly mocking.

She turned away from him as Meg appeared, trying to read the woman's expression as she too approached the table and took a pasty. Meg smiled and admired Isabel's gown, which was obviously one of her own best, and then she suddenly looked away as if she were embarrassed.

Isabel felt a little shiver of apprehension. She glanced back at Duncan.

"The lady Isabel is wondering, my dear cousin Meg, if you delivered her message to your husband last night," he said quietly. "Aren't you, my dear? Well, the message was delivered, and I've explained to our hosts the reason for your worries. They quite understood, sweetheart. Don't fret." His voice was honeyed.

"Reason?" Isabel felt herself grow pale as he stepped closer to her and put his arm solicitously round her shoulders. His fingers dug into her arm.

"Of course, sweetheart. They understand. I explained about your fall from a horse when you were a child, and that since then you have occasionally taken into your head to ride havering round the country dressed in peasant's clothes. It's a habit I had hoped you had broken, my dear; you can't go on doing it once we're married, you know. It was not Christian of your father to allow the betrothal to go ahead and not warn me of his daughter's affliction." He smiled at her with every show of grave concern.

She looked wildly at Meg, who blushed and looked away, pretending to be fiddling with the girdle of her gown, and then at Donald who gave her a sheepish smile. "There's a good lass," he murmured placatingly as though she were a horse or a dog to be gentled.

"But it's all lies," she burst out indignantly. "There's

nothing wrong with me! You must believe me!" She looked round desperately "Duncan, tell them."

He laughed. "I have told them, sweet, and they commiserate fully with my misfortune." His eyes were bright with hidden amusement. "I've explained to them that it only happens near the full of the moon. At other times you're as gentle and douce a lassie as ever a man could want for wife." He held out his hand to her. "Now come. We've overstayed our welcome and we must ride, mist or no mist. Is my horse ready, Donald? I take it you're not riding to Craig Law if it stays like this?"

The other man shrugged. "They'll not hunt in this, I'm thinking. Maybe later. I'll ride over in the forenoon and see how it goes there." He couldn't take his eyes from Isabel's face, but reluctantly he led the way towards the corner stair which led down to the ground floor.

Isabel gave one backward glance over her shoulder towards Meg, who waited by the table, and was mortified to see the woman look away and cross herself superstitiously with a visible shiver. After that she gave up. There was nothing for it but to follow Donald down the stairs with Duncan close behind her.

Once they were at the bottom of the stair there was no alternative but to allow him to lift her on to the ready-saddled horse before himself swinging up into the saddle. The door was dragged open, and raising his hand to Donald who stood beside it, he trotted the stallion out into the white mist, letting the door slam shut after them.

The fog was very thick as they trotted up the track beneath the lofty pine trees. In only minutes the tower behind them had vanished and they were alone in the white world.

They rode in complete silence, with Isabel seething quietly with fury at the trick he had played on her. At the head of the track he reined in the horse and threw back his head and laughed.

"Now I've done it. My reputation will never recover. The Black Fox tricked into a betrothal with a moon-mad maid! That was a bad mistake of yours, my lady; surely you had more sense than to try and confide in my closest kin!" He chuckled again.

"I had to try and tell someone," she retorted sulkily.

"I told you to tell no one, Isabel." His voice was suddenly harsh. "I asked you to trust me. I do not expect you to go making trouble behind my back. I shall have to see to it now that you have no further opportunity to spread rumours and lies about the countryside."

"They're not rumours and lies." She clenched her teeth angrily as he spurred the horse into a gallop. "I had to try and warn him. Don't you see . . ."

But her cry was lost in the rush of wind as the enormous hooves thundered over the mossy ground.

She closed her eyes wearily, forced to cling round his waist to prevent herself from falling, resting her cheek against his cloak which was already soaked through with moisture from the mist. It was impossible to talk, but she went on seething inwardly at every stride as they galloped across the hillside. It was impossible to tell in which direction they were riding, but this time they seemed to be following a well-marked track.

Morning was drawing on when at last the horse was steadied by Duncan's hand on his bridle. The track led steeply upwards and then sharply to the left, skirting a deep precipitous natural cauldron in the rock, the narrow path in places coming within inches of the sheer edge. The mist boiled and seethed in the depths, clearing momentarily now and then to reveal the mountainside plunging downwards towards the rocky floor far below. Somewhere nearby Isabel heard the raucous cry of a hoodie crow and she spied it, a black malevolent shape on a rock as it tore at the mangled corpse of a dead rabbit, and she shuddered.

She closed her eyes nervously, not liking even to look at the misty depths, thankful for the sure tread of Thane, and her arms tightened round Duncan's waist.

The other horseman was nearly upon them before they knew it, galloping at breakneck speed down the single track behind them. He saw them almost as he was on them and wrenched his animal to a rearing halt. Below them a cascade of shale slipped from the path and disappeared out of sight beneath the stamping hooves as the black stallion let out a whistling scream of fury.

"Crawfurd, by God! I've caught up with you." The rider was fully armed beneath his long cloak. Isabel saw the dull glint of the breastplate, the steel gauntlets on the horse's bridle.

"William?" Duncan drawled. "Why the hurry, my friend? I return to Glencarnie, as you see." He half-turned in the saddle, looking the other man up and down through heavy-lidded eyes.

"Aye, and I've stopped you in time. You still have the woman with you, I see."

Isabel, recognising the terse voice as that of one of the men in Duncan's room, guessed that this must be William Stewart. He glared at her. His hair flamed like his sister's but there was no regularity of feature, no beauty in the face she saw before her. He had a heavy red complexion and sandy eyelashes which gave his face a naked insolent look. His nose had been broken at some time and it was flattened into an ugly caricature. His eyes were unmistakably cruel.

"I caught up with her and I still have her." Duncan's voice was cool. "Follow me on, William. We'll ride on to the slopes of Ben Lairg before we talk. I've no mind to lose my horse in this devil's brew." He gestured lightly towards the misty precipice below them, but already William was urging his horse alongside, almost forcing them off the narrow track. Once the black horse's offside hoof slipped sickeningly on the edge of the path and his two riders felt his desperate scrabble before regaining his foothold.

William pushed his horse even closer. "Why are you taking her back?" he demanded, his voice rough with impatience. "She knows the plan, Margaret has told me everything. She overheard us talking. She threatened to go and warn the king."

"I know," Duncan replied curtly. "I have my own way of ensuring her silence, have no fear on that score."

"Your way was hardly effective, I hear," the other man snapped. "You allowed her to run round Cairn Dyke

telling the whole world our plans. I've just come from
there. I wanted to reach you before you set off back to
Glencarnie and I guessed you'd call on Fleming. Duncan,
if our plan is to succeed we must have total surprise. There
can be no half measures; no failure; our lives depend on
it."

"There will be no failure."

The path widened for a moment and Duncan reined in.

"This is no place for riding two abreast, William," he
repeated quietly. "Say your say and then go on ahead
of me, please. I'll not ride thigh to thigh with you
here."

"I'll say my say," William faced Duncan angrily. "The
only way to ensure her silence is to cut her throat. I'll not
have the plan ruined for the sake of a skirt and a pair of
pretty eyes."

Isabel gasped in terror.

Duncan half turned in the saddle. "Get down," he
ordered quietly, giving her his arm. "Then go and stand
over there, out of the way."

She slid to the ground and ran to the stunted thorn tree
he indicated, putting it between herself and the angry
men. Her heart was hammering in her throat in terror.

"Do the others know about her?" Duncan asked William peremptorily.

The other man nodded. "Of course they know, now.
God dammit, man, she could have betrayed the whole
plan. Listen, Donald told me at Cairn Dyke that you know
the king is here; no doubt you were riding to tell us. But
the others are already on their way south. We too heard the
king was at Craig Law, and it's a God-sent chance to get
him now; he'll be less well guarded down there and many
of the border lords are with us; we're amongst our own
people here. Besides, we must do it now. Who knows who
may have paid attention to that woman's prattle? So we
don't have much time. The others are going to meet us at a
spot about two miles north of the castle. It's lucky I rode
ahead to make sure of catching you in time. I might have
missed you in all this damned mist and there is much for us
to do today. But first, the woman." He glanced over his

shoulder towards Isabel. "I'll do it, if you've no stomach for the job."

She shrank back amongst the thorny spines, watching horrified as he dragged his heavy sword free of the scabbard. Then, purposefully, he turned his horse in her direction.

CHAPTER
TEN

"DON'T you lay a finger on her, William," Duncan shouted. "Do you not know that those who are touched in the mind are protected by God?"

William whirled. "She's not touched in the mind, Crawfurd. That's a story you made up to save yourself from her indiscretion at Cairn Dyke. She's as normal as you or I. And she's dangerous."

Isabel watched, paralysed, as again he raised his sword, turning his horse towards her. She couldn't move; she couldn't even breathe.

"I will not have her killed." Duncan's voice was like steel. "Take one step nearer her, Stewart, and it is you who will die!" There was a rasping sound as he tore his own sword from its scabbard. He wore no armour but the expression on his face was murderous enough to make Stewart reconsider. He hesitated and the two horsemen faced each other tensely for a moment, then with a sharp ugly laugh Stewart returned his sword to its resting place.

"You seem to have taken leave of your senses, Crawfurd," he snarled. "To allow a woman to threaten our plan! Very well then, she must come with us. You will have to gag her when we near Craig Law."

"We're not going to Craig Law." Duncan calmly sheathed his own weapon. "The plan is unchanged. We will not strike before the king returns north."

Stewart's face turned a deep red. "Are you out of your mind? This is a heaven-sent chance. The king has walked into a trap; we can have him dead by dusk and a new king to rule Scotland before dawn tomorrow."

"I said no." Duncan repeated the words with exaggerated patience.

"Are you a turncoat, sir?" Stewart asked suddenly, with suspicion dawning in his pale eyes. "Has this woman swayed you from our plan? Because, believe me, we're not stopping now. The others are already on their way to Craig Law. It has been decided."

Isabel saw Duncan's face darken with anger. "Why did you not consult me?"

"You had already left to look for that woman when the word came that the king was riding south. And besides, there were enough of us left at Glencarnie to make the decision. We counted hands; all were for the change of plan. You are too late to change it back." His horse was pawing the path restlessly. "Are you with us or against us, Crawfurd? Decide now."

Duncan's hand hadn't left the hilt of his sword. As Isabel watched, holding her breath, she saw him pull it free of its scabbard once more, the long blade curving in the air before him. Then she heard with a gasp of relieved joy the answer she had prayed he would give.

"Then I'm against you, Stewart. I had hoped to keep my secret a while longer till you were all in my net. You may as well know I am the king's faithful liegeman and always have been. I've been working for months to uncover your nest of vipers and I had almost succeeded. Your contacts in England I know; those in France have been harder to name – I had not expected to find traitors there."

With a vicious oath Stewart unsheathed his own weapon. Without hesitation he drove his spurs into his horse's ribs and rode at Duncan. There was a clash of sparking metal as the swords met and met again.

With a cry of fear for Duncan, Isabel ran a step or two forward as the two great horses circled one another on the narrow path, their hooves slipping in the mud at the edge of the cliff fall. Duncan wore no armour against the flailing sword of his opponent, but at the same time he was able to dodge more quickly and manoeuvre the black horse lightly from side to side. The clash of swords rang echoing in the quiet air. Her hands pressed against her mouth, Isabel retreated again behind the stunted thorn and watched the two circling figures in their shroud of thickening mist.

Stewart seemed to have the advantage at once. She saw him pressing forward, the two horses shoulder against shoulder, raising his sword high above his head. As the black took a step backwards his hind legs began to slip over the edge. Isabel heard herself scream as Duncan flung himself sideways from the saddle, landing cat-like back on the path, both hands gripping the hilt of his sword. With a colossal effort the horse, relieved of its rider's weight, clawed itself back on to the path and galloped out of sight into the mist.

Stewart whirled his own mount to face the tall, lithe figure before him, and Isabel heard him give a short hard laugh.

"So, the Black Fox's pelt too will hang at my saddle bow! My first trophy in a day of trophies!" He nudged the animal forward with his plated toe.

Duncan sprang sideways out of reach. "You'll have to get off that horse, Stewart, if you want to kill me," he panted. Again he dodged as the furious rider lunged down at him.

The path was turning into a quagmire which made him slip, but the plunging hooves found it harder to grip. With an oath Stewart flung himself from the saddle, gripping his own sword with both mailed hands. Isabel found she was shivering uncontrollably as she watched the two figures circling one another in the mist. First one and then the other grew shadowy and indistinct as thick curdled patches of fog drifted up over the lip of the rock basin beneath them.

Stewart was the stronger; he was full-accoutred and had the longer reach, but Duncan, she saw with breathless relief, was taking every advantage of his greater agility. With one flick of his wrist he had unfastened the latchet of his cloak, letting it fall in the mud so that he was completely unhampered, harrying his opponent with quick lunging movements of the sword-point.

He struck home on Stewart's breastplate with a sharp ring of metal, but though Stewart staggered backwards

the sword skidded harmlessly sideways. Then Stewart
lunged forward, catching Duncan's shoulder a glancing
blow. Bright blood showed through the slit in his doublet
and Isabel had to press her sleeve tightly against her lips to
stop herself screaming out loud once again. Duncan staggered and fell to one knee as with a yell of triumph the
armoured man closed in, sword raised.

She was almost too stunned with fright to look as
Stewart, slipping with his mailed feet in the mud, stumbled on his enemy's discarded cloak. Still half kneeling
Duncan raised his sword, taking advantage of the other
man's hesitation, and aiming just below the steel pauldron
which protected the man's shoulder, drove his blade
home.

Again it failed to pierce the armour, and slipped, but
then somehow it gained purchase, sending Stewart reeling
backwards off balance. Gasping for breath he tried to
regain his foothold, but already Duncan had leaped to his
feet and was pursuing his advantage.

With two unparried thrusts of his weapon Duncan had
pushed his opponent to the very edge of the path where the
earth was soft and crumbling. With a sudden scream
Stewart stepped backwards, missed his foothold completely, and fell.

A wreath of mist drifted silently over Duncan as he
stood breathing heavily on the narrow path. Isabel scrambled from her hiding place and ran towards him, her shoes
squelching in the mud, the breath rasping in her throat.
She stopped a few feet from him.

"Are you badly hurt?" The blood was congealing
darkly over his shirt and doublet, and a fresh red stain was
spreading through the fine linen even as she watched.

He shook his head. "It's only a flesh wound."

She bit her lip at the curt tone. She had expected
something else.

"Why didn't you tell me you were in the king's employ,
Duncan?" she asked softly, her hand for a moment touching his sleeve.

He stared down at her sternly. "I had my reasons. I
suppose you realise that months of planning have been

wasted thanks to your interference. Another week and I'd have nailed the ringleaders. Now the king is more endangered than ever."

She recoiled at the bitterness of his words. "If you had only trusted me – told me."

"Well, I didn't. I asked you to trust me, as I remember. But it's all out now, so I might as well tell you the remainder of the tale to set your mind at rest." He gave a wry smile. "It was the king's idea to use my betrothal to you as a distraction. Stewart and his friends were growing suspicious about the time I spent at court, so I had to find a reason quickly. We reckoned that introducing a Strathblair to Glencarnie would deflect their interest about me, quite apart from doing away with your father's opposition to the king. Once the plot was uncovered and the men dealt with, the king would have released me from my obligation to you."

He stooped wearily and pulled a tussock of grass to wipe the mud from his sword, then he slammed it home in its sheath.

Isabel stared at him, stunned. "You mean you never intended to marry me?" she whispered.

"No," he said. "At least, not at the beginning . . ."

She did not notice the hesitation in his voice. "And the bride wreath? The ceremony you arranged with Father Cuthbert?" she stammered. "Was that all pretence?"

He looked taken aback for a moment. "Ah, that. Yes, I admit I had thought for a while to go through with it. I had your promise, don't forget." He shrugged. "I think you had me bewitched, vixen, for a while. Be thankful circumstances brought me to my senses."

She turned away quickly, overwhelmed by the sharp feeling of desolation which swept through her. For a moment she could not bring herself to speak. Then she straightened her shoulders and looked at him again, hoping her face betrayed nothing of the turmoil inside her.

"So, what are you going to do with me now?" she asked as haughtily as she could.

He gave her a long appraising stare. Then unexpectedly he chuckled. "I dare say I could think of something, given time. But enough of this, vixen. Before anything else we have important business at Craig Law." His face was sober again. "The other conspirators are meeting there, don't forget; there is no time to lose if we are to warn the king before it's too late. I take it you're with me, now that our intentions are known to be the same?" He did not wait for her reply. Already he was looking round at the mist, searching the emptiness, a worried frown on his brow. Then, putting his fingers to his mouth, he gave a shrill whistle. A few moments later the black horse Thane trotted like an apparition out of the mist and thrust its muzzle into his hands, snorting softly. Three paces behind it was Stewart's chestnut, pecking nervously in the slippery mud. Duncan caught the reins of both. "Can you ride Stewart's horse? We'll go quicker with two."

She eyed it warily, but not for anything would she have admitted any qualms about mounting the enormous beast. "Of course I can ride it," she retorted and she stepped forward and reached for the rein.

For a brief moment she felt his hands round her waist as he lifted her to the saddle and then she was alone, trying to arrange her heavy blue skirts as best she could around the high pommel. He swung himself up on to Thane, cursing silently as he jarred his wounded shoulder, and then he spurred past her, back the way they had come, along the narrow path and then up onto the broad track across the heather.

They rode hard for what seemed like hours across the shrouded moorland, never slackening their speed, never speaking in the dense white solitude which surrounded them.

So he had never intended to marry her at all. All her fears, her attempts at escape, Andrew's involvement, and his death, had been in vain. Had she but waited quietly at Glencarnie Duncan would have released her anyway. Isabel frowned as she rode. No. Her whole being cried out against believing him. Surely his threats – and those of his mother – had been real? Marjorie's suffering, and the bottle of poison, they had been genuine enough, even he could not deny that.

But then she remembered his anger when she had told him about that. And his words "The sacred bond of motherhood will not save her if anything should happen to you . . ." after he had confronted Lady Crawfurd. Could it be that after all he had intended to return her to her father?

There was a lump in her throat as she glanced at him through her eyelashes, an indistinct figure, riding somewhat stiffly because of his shoulder a length or so ahead of her in the low cloud, and she thought again unwillingly of his kisses, his barely restrained passion. So she had bewitched him, had she? And he was thankful he'd come to his senses. She felt a sudden spurt of anger. How dare he! First he frightened her, then he mocked her, then he swore at her for not trusting him and then on top of all that he had the effrontery to tell her that he had never had any intention of marrying her anyway!

She brushed her hand angrily across her eyes. She should be heartily glad of that. It was not as though she had ever liked him. Any passing attraction he might have had was purely madness on her part. She was relieved to find he was no traitor or murderer, yes, and she was thankful that he had risked everything to save her and kill Stewart when he could have let the man spit her on his sword and saved his secret, but more than that, never. As a person, she told herself firmly, she despised and hated him and it was an unmitigated relief that once the king had been duly warned and the miscreants brought to justice she would be able to return home to Strathblair and never see him again.

Her tumbling thoughts were interrupted as ahead of her Duncan raised his hand at last, bringing his horse to a halt.

"We're about half a mile from the place where they had planned to meet," he said quietly. "I don't know if there was a time arranged – it's hard to tell the hour at all in this accursed fog, but we'll skirt round the back of the hill to miss them just in case and come to Craig Law from the west."

His face was lined with strain and she saw that his shoulder had started bleeding again. Fresh blood stained

the front of his shirt, but she restrained the exclamation of
sympathy which immediately sprang to her lips. He was
strong. No doubt it would add to his standing with the
king if he arrived wounded at Craig Law.

She followed him silently, guiding the big chestnut off
the track into the thick heather. She was cold and completely exhausted, for they had been riding for several
hours and the damp had seeped through her clothing to
her skin; her hands, clutching the ornate reins, were
frozen stiff, but never would she admit any such weakness
to him.

She couldn't think how Duncan could find his way so
surely in the fog; she had been lost from the moment they
set out in the morning from Cairn Dyke, but she had no
doubt at all that they were exactly where he said they were
and she strained her ears nervously for the sound of other
riders near by.

Duncan was obviously doing the same, for after a few
hundred yards he rode alongside her and took her rein,
bringing both horses to a standstill, his finger to his
lips. She stared round, shivering. Had he heard something?

The white silence beat down round them in a palpable
wall, and after motioning her to stay quiet he gently urged
the two horses on almost at once, still holding her rein. All
around them there were the tiny sounds of dripping moisture and the gentle trickle of running water from hidden
runnels in the heather.

Then, distantly, she heard a muffled shout.

He reined in again abruptly and stood up in his stirrups
to see better, but it was no use. The white blanketing wall
had closed about them if anything more thickly than
before, and shaking his head he nudged the horses slowly
on.

They made a large circle across the heather in the fog
and rejoined the track some half-mile further on without
seeing or hearing anything else. To Isabel all was the same
strange wilderness of fog and heather, but Duncan's sense
of direction was acute. He brought them unerringly back
to their path and before long, to her intense relief, Isabel

saw, a black shadow in the distance, the looming bulk of
Craig Law Castle behind its walls, a banner hanging limply from its flagstaff, a ghostly shadow in a sea of white on
the tower.

Duncan cantered ahead alone to speak to the guards at
the outer wall of the castle. She reined in and watched him
lean forward in his saddle talking to the men, wearily
trying to ease the pain in his shoulder, and then she saw
him jerk upright in surprise.

"What!" She heard his exclamation ring out in the
silence. "We're too late, then. Call some men, quickly,
and follow me. Pray God we're in time!"

He tore the horse round as the guard began shouting
orders to men unseen in the guardhouse. Lights flared and
there was a ring of arms and the clatter of hooves and the
noise of men shouting.

"What is it? What's happened?" Isabel called nervously
as he thundered back towards her.

"The king has left. They sent him a message – some
trick – and he was fooled by it!" he shouted at her, lashing
the stallion into a gallop as he tore past her up the track
with a hastily mounted detachment of men already galloping after him from the castle.

She dragged her bucking horse out of their path and
tried to soothe it, trembling. She would only be in the way
if she followed, and anyway already the track was empty –
white with drifting mist as the drum of hoofbeats grew
muffled and died away.

She sat still for only a moment longer and then she
turned the horse down the slope towards the castle. It was
all out of her hands now. She had probably spoiled everything for Duncan and the king might die now because of
her, but there was nothing she could do – nothing except
ride into Craig Law and wait.

The shadowy figures were round her in a second. One
moment she was alone in the mist and the next two men
were at her bridle, whilst a third held a sword at her throat.
She stifled a cry.

"Not a sound, lady, if you value your life." A gruff

voice came to her out of the murk. She found herself
looking down into a pair of fierce brown eyes. The face
changed abruptly, registering astonishment.

"Isabel of Strathblair!"

"Murdoch!" She swallowed nervously.

His sword didn't waver but momentarily he glanced
back. "Stay still, men," he called. "This is the Black Fox's
woman. Is he here then?" He addressed her gruffly. "He
didn't come to the meeting place at the appointed time
with Stewart."

She stiffened. So Murdoch was one of them – a rebel
and a traitor. She tried to think steadily, wondering if they
had heard the horses leaving the castle. It seemed
unlikely.

"Duncan told me to wait here, out of the way," she said
nervously. "He said he had to meet someone. We got lost
in the fog and we couldn't tell the time of day, it was so
thick up on the moors."

Why were they here, near the castle? Could it be that the
king had ridden off in the wrong direction after all and
missed them, she wondered, murmuring under her breath
a fervent prayer that this was so.

But the next moment he dashed her hopes. "We didn't
wait for him, but I daresay he'll run into the rest of the
party – they waited at the appointed place for the king and
no doubt they'll have him by now." He gave an unpleasant
laugh. "Crawfurd will kick himself if he misses the killing,
but that's his fault."

"I thought William Stewart said this woman would
betray us?" Another voice, authoritative and deep, spoke
from the shadows, and she saw two other figures behind
the first.

She held her breath.

"Maybe, but she belongs to the Black Fox," Murdoch's
voice was smooth. "Good or bad, it's for him to deal with
her. She must be with us or he would hardly have brought
her here. But now she is here she can help us get into the
castle. No one would suspect a woman. Come on. Not
another sound until I say so!"

The group of men moved cautiously forward, leading

her horse with them. The sword was pointing at her heart.
Isabel's mouth had gone dry with fear. She could see silent
figures creeping round the base of the wall inside the moat
and it seemed as if the guard had ridden out and left the
castle completely unattended. In another moment they
would be in and the castle itself would fall to the rebels.
She wanted to scream a warning but she was paralysed
with fear.

At the first ring of her horse's hooves on the hollow
drawbridge a challenge rang out, however. She drew breath
sharply as the sword pricked her through her cloak.

"Answer," Murdoch hissed. "Answer. Tell them who
you are."

Isabel swallowed. "It is I," she called, her voice husky
with fright. "Isabel Douglass of Strathblair."

She could see the shadowy braziers in the courtyard
itself now and the figures of two or three lounging men.
Three guards alone seemed to stand between her and the
castle entrance, and though they had their swords in their
hands they were relaxed, standing at ease, not suspecting
anything.

Somehow she had to warn them, and yet she had no
doubt that as soon as she drew breath to shout again that
icy steel would thrust home between her ribs. She could
still feel it touching her skin and she had the feeling that
Murdoch would enjoy pushing it home.

Her horse threw up its head nervously and let out a
piercing whinny. She gasped and patted it, feeling the fine
chestnut skin warm and damp across its withers as it
shivered beneath her gentle caress.

Only a few more paces and they would be across the
bridge and under the gatehouse itself. Taking a deep
breath she rested her forefinger and thumb against its
neck, stroking it, then gently she gripped a fold of the fine
skin. She glanced at the man at her side. The horse had
hidden his sword from the eyes of the first guard who had
watched them pass with incurious eyes. Murdoch's gaze
was focused on the castle entrance but the sword point
hadn't wavered.

She took a deep breath and with all her strength viciously twisted the fold of the horse's skin. As a distraction it worked better than she could ever have hoped. The animal exploded beneath her, rearing and bucking furiously, knocking Murdoch and his sword sideways against the bridge rail.

Isabel screamed, clinging to the saddle, her eyes shut, calling again and again for help. It was the last thing she remembered. The panicking horse, twisting beneath her, dislodged her from the saddle and she flew off, landing heavily on the cobblestones beneath the gateway.

She lay quite still, unconscious of the furious fighting which was suddenly going on on every side of her, and of the man who ran forward and dragged her from beneath the flailing chestnut hooves and carried her, running, towards the safety of the guardroom.

When she came round she was lying on a bench and someone was gently sponging her face with cold water. Her whole body felt bruised and stiff and she was dazed, not remembering what had happened. Nearby a torch burned in the sconce on the wall, smoking bitterly in the draught, and it dazzled her eyes. She raised her hand to shade them.

"What happened?" she murmured. "Where am I?"

A strong hand took hers and held it. "You saved the castle, vixen."

She focused slowly on the dark saturnine face which had appeared close to her own. His eyes were alight with golden glints but his expression was very grave.

"The king?" she asked slowly, trying to remember. "The king?"

"The king is safe. We reached him in time and we have the rebels." He spoke with grim satisfaction.

"Murdoch, he was there," she said faintly, remembering the prick of the sword.

"Aye, he was there, and he paid for it with his life," he replied grimly, "as did many of them."

"Except for the ones I ruined your hope of catching." She made a rueful face and winced, trying to ease her aching bruises.

He grinned. "I'll catch them anyway. It'll be a pleasure making some of my prisoners talk, that I promise. But you must rest, sweetheart." He leaned forward and gently sponged her face again. She saw that there was blood on the cloth and, bewildered, she raised her shaking fingers to her forehead.

"Did I fall off the horse?" she asked, puzzled. "I remember now. I wanted him to rear. It was the only way I could think of to take me out of the reach of Murdoch's sword, so I pinched the horse. But I don't remember anything after that."

Duncan gave a shout of laughter. "You pinched a full-blooded war-horse? Only a woman would think of that! Can you wonder that he threw you! He must have wondered what kind of harridan he had on his back. No," gently he pushed her back as she struggled to raise herself on to her elbow. "Don't try and get up yet. You're badly hurt."

She didn't argue. Her head had started throbbing as soon as she moved and she felt sick and dizzy as she closed her eyes. Dimly she heard a woman's voice:

"Is she fit to be moved, Sir Duncan? We have a room for her upstairs. The queen has given orders for the court physician to attend her there."

"I'll bring her." His voice swam, coming and going, in the distance.

She felt his arms ease round her as gently as if she had been a baby so as not to hurt her and he lifted her until her head was lying against his chest. For a moment she felt a wave of tremendous relief and happiness sweep over her and then all went black again.

When she awoke the sun was shining through the window of a small chamber hung with rich tapestries. She found that she was lying naked beneath covers of silk and rich fur. She stretched luxuriously and then winced as she felt her bruises once more. At once someone was at her side.

"My lady, are you awake?" A girl was leaning over her. "Do you feel better?"

She nodded, raising herself on her elbow and looking about her. The girl ran to a side table and came back with a cup of warm wine which she sipped gratefully.

Then she began to remember.

Slowly the events of the previous day came back, swimming up out of the depths of her mind. She looked around vaguely, watching the girl as she busied herself over a chest of linen in the corner, shaking out a finely worked shift and laying it across a stool.

How long had she been here in this bed? She remembered riding; riding through the mist, endlessly following another horse, straining her eyes so as not to lose sight of it in the whiteness. And she remembered the anxiety, the hurry, the castle at last looming in the distance. She frowned, rubbing the back of her hand against her aching head. There was a fall, and pain and the clash of arms and shouting, and then Duncan bending over her, sponging her face, his own so close to hers, and then the feel of his strong arms round her as he had lifted her so gently from the bench in the guardhouse, and in the moment before she lost consciousness the whispered touch of his lips on her hair.

With a little smile she took another sip from the cup in her hands, and then she lay back, thinking about Duncan.

The maid had been watching her drink. "When you feel well enough, my lady, the king wants to see you. He wants to thank you himself for what you did. You saved the castle, you know." She smiled admiringly, holding out her hand for the cup. "I've put fresh clothes on the coffer here, my lady."

Isabel sat up hastily. She could not keep the king waiting, and apart from her aches and bruises she felt quite rested now. Slowly she pushed her legs out from beneath the covers and felt for the floor with her feet.

The girl helped her to dress, easing the soft, rich garments over Isabel's aching shoulders, then she produced an ivory-backed brush and set to work on Isabel's long tangled hair. She had succeeded at last in smoothing it into a silken wing across the girl's shoulders when the door opened abruptly and a woman walked in.

With a gasp of surprise the maid dropped a deep curtsey, and Isabel, rising unsteadily from the stool in front of
the dressing table, followed suit. There was no mistaking
the attractive figure or the strange accent of King James's
English Queen, Joan, whom she had seen but once in the
distance at the evening meal at Linlithgow.

"So, are you better, child?" she asked in a low, musical
voice. "I hear that we owe everything to your courage.
Glencarnie has told the king of your steadfast determination to warn him of the plot and of the heroic way you
warned the guards at the castle gate."

Isabel blushed a deep pink. "I am only happy that you
are all safe, ma'am," she murmured shyly.

The Queen held out her hand with a smile. "Come, let
the girl finish dressing your hair. Then you must come
down. My husband wants to speak to you himself."

She waited smiling quietly whilst the maid deftly
braided Isabel's hair and pinned on an elaborate headdress
and veil, then she turned and herself led Isabel out of the
room into a narrow passage which led to the broad newel
stair. Together they went down, with the Queen steadying
Isabel as she hesitated on the stairs, still a little dizzy from
her fall as she walked.

The Great Hall where the king was waiting was crowded
any emotion as she followed the Queen to the dais and
led her towards the dais at the far end. The king was
resplendent in a jewelled gown with an ornate collar of
gold, and beside him stood the austere figure of the Black
Fox.

Duncan's sharp eyes saw her at once, but he didn't show
any emotion as she followed the Queen to the dais and
curtseyed deeply to the king; and she in her turn did not
dare raise her eyes to the man who stood silently at her
sovereign's side.

"So." James drew her close to him. "The daughter of
Strathblair. I owe you much, it seems, lassie. You have my
deepest gratitude for what you did."

She blushed as the king swivelled round in his chair and
squinted up at the inscrutable figure beside him.

"We must reward you both, but tell me, Glencarnie,

why are you and this young lady not yet married? Wasn't it my express order that you should be wed?" He frowned.

Isabel caught her breath, her eyes fixed on Duncan's face. He smiled easily. "There was something of a delay in the proceedings, sir," he said blandly. "Lady Isabel, it seemed, felt unable to comply with your grace's instructions until she had undertaken a certain amount of sewing and I felt duty bound to respect her wishes in the matter."

"Is that so?" The king swung back to her. He was smiling broadly.

"So, you decided to put off the evil hour like a second Penelope, eh?" he teased.

Duncan gave a short laugh. "I think, sir, that you fathom the lady's intentions exactly."

Isabel was looking from one to the other, bewildered. What did they mean? They were talking as though the wedding really had been intended after all, and yet, surely, Duncan had told her that he had had no intention of going through with it. She found herself looking wistfully in his direction, but he had turned away to fetch a goblet of wine for the king.

"Leave the child alone, you two," Joan's voice suddenly broke in at her elbow. She indicated a low stool. "Sit down, my dear. You must take some wine too, and some food. I can see you're still weak from your fall." She took her place in her chair next to her husband's, and Isabel sank gratefully on to the stool at the Queen's feet.

She felt Duncan's eyes on her at last and she looked up eagerly. He winked and watched as she accepted the wine that was brought to her and sipped it slowly.

The king was watching her too. "I've a mind to have the wedding today," he said thoughtfully ."Yes. Glencarnie, you shall have a wife before the sun goes down. There's been too much delay in this alliance already, and it will give us a chance for a double celebration."

Isabel felt her heart beginning to beat faster "Your grace . . ." she stammered breathlessly, but she was cut short by Duncan.

"No, sir."

The king raised an eyebrow. "No, Sir Duncan?"

"No, sir. You said I should have the choice of nullifying the agreement once my work for you was done. I am exercising that choice. Lady Isabel has made it more than clear that she does not wish for the match." His face was harsh and very proud.

She gasped, looking at him in dismay, and almost, for a moment, she spoke. Then her own pride got the better of her and she drew herself upright, setting her goblet down on the side table near her. Duncan should never know how nearly she had come to admitting at last that she loved him. He had made it clear he wanted none of her, and that was the end of it. Her lovely face shuttered with pain, she looked away from him.

But the Queen had been watching her closely, and with a hidden smile she suddenly stood up. "Sir Duncan, this cannot be decided so fast and so publicly. You and the lady Isabel must have the chance to talk this over alone. Take her up on to the battlements; talk there."

Duncan looked surprised and Isabel saw his lips tighten in displeasure, but even he could not disobey the queen. He stepped forward and gave her and the king a brief bow. "If you think I should, ma'am," he said shortly, "though I doubt if the lady and I have anything else to say to each other on the subject." Without looking at Isabel he strode past her and led the way briskly out of the hall.

They walked together in silence up the long spiralling staircase which led to the roof of the keep. The door at the top was open.

Isabel gasped involuntarily as she saw the bright sunlight flooding over the grey stone. She had almost forgotten that the world could be anything but a sea of white mist as she glanced down towards the surrounding countryside, which glowed warm and brown and golden beneath the dazzling blue of the sky.

Above them the royal lion floated and rippled at the flagstaff, straining on the golden field with his rearing claws. On four sides of the keep the lookouts kept their station, patrolling the battlements, their eyes trained on the distance, ignoring the man and the woman who strolled across the roof leads towards a sheltered corner. She found her heart was thumping uncontrollably as he stopped and turned to face her at last. She could not meet his eyes.

After a short silence she swallowed nervously. "What did you mean about Penelope?" she asked softly, resting her hands on the sunwarmed battlements. "Who was she?"

He smiled grimly. "She was a lady in Greek legend who made a promise to marry when she had finished weaving a tapestry. Each day she sat down to weave, and each night she crept down to the loom and unravelled every thread."

"Oh." Her voice was flat. "And you think that's what I intended?"

He gave a mirthless laugh. "I know it. The king will release you from your betrothal, Isabel. You are free now." He looked down at her, his face once again the expressionless mask she had come to know so well.

She ran her tongue nervously across her dry lips. "I don't want to be free," she whispered piteously, her voice so quiet he had to bend to hear her words. "I love you. But perhaps you don't want me . . ."

She did not dare look up at his face. For a moment he said nothing. Somewhere nearby she could hear the chatter and whistle of busy starlings in the trees and closer at hand the measured tread of one of the sentries as he paced slowly up and down the battlement behind them. Then suddenly Duncan's arms were round her.

She gasped with pain as his hands touched her bruises but she didn't notice as her lips were crushed against his. For a long time she knew nothing except the exquisite joy of being in his arms, her blood racing with the excitement of his touch. Then at last he held her away from him and his features relaxed into that elusive smile she had remembered so often.

"I left your poor maid trying to teach herself to sew in the Drum Tower," he murmured wickedly. "Will you give the girl the order to stop if I take you home to Glencarnie?"

She nodded wordlessly and he grinned again. "My mother will welcome you this time, sweetheart – as she leaves for the dower house – that I promise you, and Margaret will by now have been arrested by the king's men. So I think on this occasion you will find a better welcome in my home than you did before. But are you sure you know what you're saying, vixen? There's still time to change your mind."

"I'm sure, Fox," she replied and she raised her lips again to his.

Don't miss these exciting Masquerade Historicals!

18. The Damask Rose by Polly Meyrick

A vastly entertaining tale of an impoverished governess suddenly thrust into the teeming world of Regency London and thrown headfirst into the mad whirl of parties, balls…and love.

19. Joanna by Patricia Ormsby

In Regency London the vicious, rejected suitor of a spirited Irish girl threatens to ruin her reputation. And not only is her good name at stake but her very life, as well!

20. The Passionate Puritan by Belinda Grey

Her Puritan upbringing hadn't prepared her for this! Her hand in marriage virtually sold to an arrogant Royalist, Abigail finds her conscience at war with her traitorous heart.

21. The Crescent Moon by Shirley Grey

A fascinating tale of intrigue unfolds in the court of France's King Henri II, as a beautiful young gentlewoman battles tremendous odds to be with the man she loves.

22. Man of Consequence by Jane Wilby

An amusing and delightful story of a very foolish brother and sister who, when let loose in the straitlaced London society of the early nineteenth century, nearly bring themselves to ruin.

23. Dear Lover England by Pamela Bennetts

The deceptively fragile hand of Elizabeth I of England manipulates the destinies of everyone around her—including that of her beautiful but strangely tormented maid of honor.

These titles may be available at your local bookstore.

Masquerade
HISTORICAL ROMANCES

Suspense...mystery...intrigue...history
but most of all...love

Let MASQUERADE historical romances take
you places you've never been, eras you've
only imagined...Elizabethan England,
Napoleonic France, Renaissance Italy,
and many more.

Take a journey into the past and
thrill to the joys and sorrows of
people in love in times gone by.

It will be a journey you'll never forget.